DATE			

W9-BNH-433

Collateral
Damage

Also by Michael Bowen

Collateral Damage

MICHAEL BOWEN

ST. MARTIN'S PRESS ❧ NEW YORK

COLLATERAL DAMAGE. Copyright © 1999 by Michael
Bowen. All rights reserved. Printed in the United States
of America. No part of this book may be used or repro-
duced in any manner whatsoever without written permission except in the case of brief quotations embodied
in critical articles or reviews. For information, address St.
Martin's Press, 175 Fifth Avenue, New York, N.Y. 10010.

Library of Congress Cataloging-in-Publication Data

Bowen, Michael.
    Collateral damage / Michael Bowen. — 1st ed.
       p. cm.
    ISBN 0-312-20289-X
    I. Title.
    PS3552.O864C65   1999
    813'.54—dc21   99-21331
                                                        CIP

First Edition: June 1999

10 9 8 7 6 5 4 3 2 1

For JAB, MJB, and JHB, who someday will understand

Calvert Manor

Second Floor

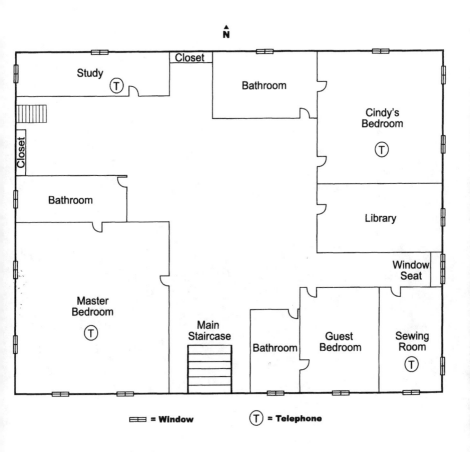

N

Study (T)	**Closet**
	Bathroom
Closet	**Cindy's Bedroom** (T)
Bathroom	
	Library
Master Bedroom (T)	**Window Seat**
Main Staircase	**Bathroom** **Guest Bedroom** **Sewing Room** (T)

⊟⊟ = **Window**   (T) = **Telephone**

Collateral Damage

One

If you've ever heard the Buddy Morrow Orchestra play "Night Train," you can form a perfect mental image of Cindy Shepherd walking into the living room at Calvert Manor. That at least was the opinion of Richard Michaelson, who had.

Cindy's heel-clicking strut across sixty-five feet of parquet floor ended at the larger of two Chippendale writing tables, where she parked a derriere shrink-wrapped in DKNY basic black. Tipping over a discreetly tasteful THANK YOU FOR NOT SMOKING sign, she flicked ash from a Cohiba Panatela onto its back. After a delicate puff followed by a languid exhalation over her right shoulder, she surveyed the other four people in the room, whose conversation had pretty much stopped since her entrance.

"Please," she said innocently, "don't mind me."

Marjorie Randolph, who with Richard Michaelson was half of those people, wouldn't have called Cindy beautiful, though she certainly enjoyed the artless prettiness of youth. Her oval face seemed luminous in the late-morning light, which played capriciously off highlights in her chestnut hair. A yellow, amply cut man's dress shirt tried without notable success to make the least of her ample breasts, while emphasizing a waist that in someone a few years older might have suggested either anorexia or a serious acquaintance with cocaine. What would turn heads most days on Connecticut Avenue, though, was an in-your-face éclat that she effortlessly projected.

"Trust me, Cindy," said Catherine Shepherd, who had been showing Marjorie and Michaelson through the house. "You would have had our undivided attention even without the cigar."

"I know," Cindy said. Then, turning toward Marjorie and Michaelson, she added, "Valued prospects, right? Has Cathy asked for your earnest money yet? Make her give you a receipt."

"This is my sister, Cindy," Catherine explained. Her tone suggested much-put-upon but still indulgently amused patience. "Cindy, Marjorie Randolph and Richard Michaelson. They're taking a preliminary look at Calvert Manor for someone else."

"Whoever it is, *please* make them buy it," Cindy entreated earnestly. "Whatever the trustee's asking. Cindy gets a condo in Washington Harbor, Cathy and Preston get married, Preston takes Cathy on a honeymoon someplace where people think steel-gray turtlenecks are a fashion statement, and your friend gets a house Katharine Hepburn and Cary Grant could have made a movie in."

Michaelson glanced reflexively at Preston Demarest, who was wearing a steel-gray turtleneck sweater underneath a teal-blue cotton broadcloth dress shirt. Demarest had accompanied Catherine while she showed the house and was now standing a few feet away from her. He smiled gamely at Cindy's comment.

"Handsome" didn't even start to do justice to Demarest.

2

Apparently in his late twenties or early thirties, he was about six feet tall. Hair with the fiery brilliance of brand-new copper wire rolled in perfect waves across his head. Solid but unostentatious muscles rippled with casual power underneath his *GQ* ensemble. Whatever the adjectival form of "hunk" was, Michaelson reflected, Demarest qualified.

"I'm pretty sure the cigar is a new touch," Catherine told Marjorie and Michaelson. "You shouldn't have to worry about carpets and curtains stinking of stale smoke. I have that right, don't I, Cindy? I don't think I've even seen you with cigarettes since you went on your health Nazi kick in high school."

"All true," Cindy sighed as blue-gray smoke wafted toward the ceiling. "It's like riding a bicycle, though. You never really forget how."

"On the topic of trustees and offers," interjected Michaelson, who found the smoking habits of twenty-somethings less than enthralling, "what is the asking price these days?"

"The last number I heard from the trustee is two-six," Demarest said after Cindy rolled her eyes cluelessly and Catherine hesitated. "That was two months ago, and it may have changed."

"Go," Cindy commanded as she hustled over to Demarest and tried to turn him toward the door. "Update. Now. Phone in the den. 555-9113. I'd call myself but Miss Tightass doesn't take me seriously. For some reason. Just tell her secretary you've got the first live one for Calvert Manor in six weeks. She'll be on the line before the elevator music starts."

"Coming?" Demarest asked Michaelson as he gave good-natured ground before Cindy's girlish but insistent shoves.

"I don't see any civilized alternative," Michaelson said.

3

"I apologize for that little performance," Catherine said to Marjorie as the other three left the room. "Cindy likes to be on."

"She seems extremely anxious to sell."

"I can't blame her," Catherine said. She patted light brown hair as her café-au-lait eyes darted away from Marjorie's. "Mom hasn't set foot in the house since she and Dad divorced twelve years ago. Now that Dad's dead and Cindy's finished college, the home just doesn't make sense as a place for us to live. When Cindy turns twenty-four she comes into her full share of the inheritance under Dad's will. Half the value of this home makes that a bigger number. And until it's sold, taxes, upkeep, and utility bills have to be paid out of the income on the legacy."

Marjorie glanced at the enormous fireplace dominating the far end of the room, its stones hewn eighty years before Jefferson was born and its first ashes swept by slaves when the last Stuart king still ruled both England and America.

"Everything you say makes sense," Marjorie admitted, "but it's a beautiful old place with remarkable character. History and modern plumbing is a rare and appealing combination."

"Agreed," Catherine said. "But I can't see Preston and me rattling around in here after we're married. And this certainly isn't Cindy or C-Sharp's idea of an appropriate venue."

"C-Sharp?"

"His real name is Howie Kestrel. C-Sharp is his street name or stage name or something. Guitarist and lead vocalist with a D.C. rock group. Cindy has a kind of thing for naughty boys, and C-Sharp does his best to qualify."

Again Catherine broke eye contact. Marjorie sensed a current of understanding and empathy passing between her and the younger woman. When Catherine explained how sensible it was to sell the home she'd grown up in, the place where she'd practiced piano and romped with a father she'd never see again, the words sounded hollow. Catherine struck Marjorie as twenty-five going on forty. She'd swung through the house like a prim apprentice matron, seemingly avid for a suburban life ordered around soccer car pools and Suzuki practice. Her poise and understated elegance could have made her as physically striking as her younger sister, but her no-nonsense hairstyle, Laura Ashley dress, and minimal makeup all screamed SENSIBLE! instead.

She was engaged to a guy who could model Jockey briefs, and she was apparently in line for enough money to live comfortably without any heavy lifting. What Marjorie saw in Catherine Shepherd's eyes when she managed to catch them, however, didn't suggest the serenity or joie de vivre you'd expect from such happy circumstances. It wasn't that Catherine seemed miserable or desperate. There was just something superficial and unconvincing about her contentment, like the perkiness of a pledge mistress during rush week.

"The asking price is still two million six hundred thousand," Michaelson announced when he led the others back into the room roughly two hundred seconds later. "Subject to auction in the event of simultaneous qualified offers, and to approval by all interested parties. Ms. Wilcox, which turns out to be the trustee's name, was quite emphatic about that. No one's pinning anything on her."

"Naturally," Cindy said. "If she cared as much about closing a sale as she does about covering her oversized butt, we'd have moved this shack months ago."

"Well," Marjorie said with a note of finality, "that number has several more digits than my MasterCard limit, but Patrice Helmsing is in an entirely different tax bracket. I'll report to her and get back to you promptly. Thank you so much for showing us this lovely home."

*   *   *

"You didn't turn around for one last look at the place before we got in the car," Michaelson said a couple of
minutes later as Marjorie swung her Buick Regal out of
Calvert Manor's long, sloping driveway.

"I have the image indelibly imprinted on my memory,"
she said a little wistfully. "Red brick and white clapboard.
Real brick instead of brick facing and real wood instead of
aluminum siding. A roofed verandah on all four sides that
would go with mint juleps in May and Tom and Jerries in
December. An interior full of nooks, paneled basement
rooms, and other things realtors dream about. Twenty
minutes from the British embassy on a good day, but rural
Maryland once you're through the hedge gate. Even if Patrice doesn't buy it, I'll always appreciate your telling me
about this place after Avery Phillips mentioned it to you."

"His description of Calvert Manor made it sound a lot
more like you than him."

"Extra credit for insight. Patrice has been looking for a
place like this for years. It would mean the world to her
to live here. But aren't you feeling some pangs of remorse
about using Phillips's own lead against him?"

"Not in the slightest," Michaelson said. "Phillips told
me he had an interest in the house and asked me to be his
stalking horse. I said no. He didn't ask for any promises
about keeping things to myself and I didn't offer him any.
He presumably wasn't expecting me to enter the market
on a State Department pension, but he's a big boy and his
expectations are his own responsibility."

"What a splendidly cold-blooded way to put it. Do you
and Phillips go way back or anything gut-wrenching like
that?"

"I knew him in the seventies when he was a marine and
I was a deputy chief of mission. His title was military attaché, but the CIA station chief always seemed to find out

6

what Phillips learned before I did. Respect, yes; warm and fuzzy, no."

"How did he go from military intelligence to Washington real estate?" Marjorie asked.

"Something happened that left him with a knee unsuited to marine officer duties. I'm not sure what. The official record discusses the incident without obsessive attention to detail."

"Phillips can't be buying the house for himself. Did he tell you whom he's representing?"

"The European Union," Michaelson said. "He told me that he'd been approached to buy Calvert Manor for conversion into a trade mission for the bureaucrats in Brussels who run what most Americans still think of as the Common Market."

"If that got out and the trustee has any brains, it would raise the asking price considerably," Marjorie said.

"Hence his desire to use me as a cat's-paw."

"If I'd had any qualms, that would eliminate them. Calvert Manor is a home to be lived in by human beings who'll love it and care for it. It's obscene to think of it being chopped up into a rats' warren of improvised offices for *fonctionnaires*."

"I don't think there's much risk of that, for what it's worth," Michaelson said. "Calvert Manor is politically impossible for the European Union. I intend to explain that to him and suggest that he stop wasting his time on it."

"Impossible why?"

"As the protocol officers at State are fond of saying, it's a matter of appearances but appearances matter. Calvert Manor looks a lot more like an embassy than like any sensible European's idea of a trade mission."

"So what?" Marjorie asked.

"Governments have embassies. Trade groups have offices—preferably spartan offices. Every nationalist in Europe is already convinced that the Eurocrats are trying to set themselves up as a sovereign, federal government. If the EU starts doing its U.S. business in something that looks like Government House in India during the British Raj, Tories all over the continent will be yelling bloody murder. Once someone with a liter or two of political judgment over in Brussels sees a picture of Calvert Manor, Phillips's little deal will be dead in the water."

"That's very reassuring," Marjorie said. "But I wouldn't stake next month's payroll on sound political judgment in Brussels or anywhere else. I'm betting Patrice and I are going to have a fight on our hands."

A prospect so bracing that, as Marjorie realized later, it didn't occur to her to ask Michaelson why he was going to bother explaining anything to Avery Phillips.

Two

Twenty-five minutes later Michaelson unlocked a steel box fitted into the lower drawer of his desk at the Brookings Institution—the Massachusetts Avenue headquarters for the eastern establishment's permanent shadow cabinet. He took out a battered, mustard-colored, nine-by-twelve envelope. Although the date he'd written on the envelope the night he got it—2/23/94—lay some five years in the past, the envelope was on top of the files in the box because he'd dug it out the day before, just after Phillips's provocative phone call.

"Richard, I need a favor," Phillips had said a little over thirty hours earlier. "For you a potentially lucrative favor."

"Perhaps, if it doesn't involve lying, cheating, or stealing."

"How do you feel about two out of three?"

Inside the envelope was a photograph of a hotel bill lying at a slight angle against the background of a different document featuring faded, elaborately old-fashioned handwriting. (Photograph, not photocopy, for Michaelson noticed a slight distortion in the printed letters, suggesting an enlargement made from a much smaller negative.) On June 13, 1987, apparently, a traveler had checked out of the St. Demetrius Hotel in Jessenice, Yugoslavia. The charge for two nights, three room-service meals, and one long-distance call had run to just under $450. The exiting guest had settled the bill with an American Express card issued to Imex Tradco, Inc.

Not quite seven years later, on February 23, 1994, a lawyer named Josh Logan had handed Michaelson the envelope during a reception at the Indian embassy. He had accompanied this tender with the none-too-comfortable explanation that "Jim Halliburton asked me to get this to you if anything happened."

"Has something happened?" Michaelson had asked.

"He was admitted to Bethesda Naval Hospital at four o'clock this afternoon with nervous exhaustion."

"Nervous exhaustion" in Washington is a multipurpose diagnosis that can mean anything from attempted suicide to an aversion to subpoenas. In Halliburton's case, coming three months after his resignation from the White House staff, it had meant acute and apparently permanent neurasthenia; for in the years that had passed from that evening to this afternoon, Halliburton had never seen his home again.

Michaelson, in his early sixties and retired for several years from the Foreign Service, was thirteen years younger than Halliburton. Michaelson had served as everything from desk officer for Ceylon (now Sri Lanka) to deputy chief of mission for the American embassy in New Delhi, before ultimately becoming Area Director for Near East and South Asian Affairs. He had crossed paths frequently with Halliburton, who had specialized in the same part of the world for the State Department until he joined the

White House staff in the mid-eighties. That move had made Michaelson and Halliburton de facto rivals, for part of the job of each had become keeping a wary and confrontational eye on the other. (Congress didn't stumble over Ollie North's escapades all by itself.)

Michaelson handled the envelope with a practiced deftness that spared the little finger on his left hand. He had been without half of that finger ever since a heavily orchestrated late-seventies embassy riot whose participants had included an enthusiastic (but apparently nearsighted) chap with a Kalyshnikov assault rifle.

Aside from his seventy-four inches in height, the slightly maimed finger was Michaelson's only remarkable physical feature. Dark brown eyes dominated his face, looking almost black because of the contrast with his white hair. His expressions usually covered the narrow range suggested by Talleyrand's *mot* about the perfectly trained diplomat: *surtout, pas trop de zèle.* Detached, professorial interest, polite skepticism, dispassionate curiosity, gentle irony, or qualified approval were all that untrained observers were likely to read in his face or hear in his voice. The most important attribute produced by his training and experience was something that those who didn't know him well spotted only rarely, and then in such bracing form that they were often shocked. This was the ability to look the truth in the face, no matter how appalling it generally was, and to accept it dispassionately without kidding himself.

The beginning and end of the Cold War served as nearly perfect bookends for Michaelson's thirty-five eventful years as a Foreign Service officer. Stalin was still in power when Michaelson took the Foreign Service entrance examination, and the Berlin Wall had only a few years left to stand when he retired. In between he had been shot at twice that he knew of, counting the ricochet that cost him half a pinkie. Three times in a U.S. mission where he was in functional command he had ordered destruction of code books, which is the last thing you do before you turn things over to the marines. He had never turned things over to the marines.

He had established and for a few years run the State Department's Interagency Liaison Office, which was Foggy Bottom's first grudging admission that institutional survival required it to spy systematically on the CIA. (Michaelson had once commented that the Central Intelligence Agency's only deficiencies were a weakness in local geography and a problem with basic arithmetic: It thought that the Department of State was located in Langley, Virginia, and that the country had only one branch of government.) In the early seventies he had told President Nixon that India would beat Pakistan in a war. President Nixon hadn't wanted to hear that, which was bad, and the event had proved Michaelson correct, which was worse.

He had taken early retirement as a calculated gamble. While occupying an office at Brookings with other members of the government-in-waiting (or government-in-exile), he would write thin books and closely reasoned op-ed pieces; he would participate in symposiums; he would talk to reporters who wanted more than sound bites; he would mentor monographs on international affairs. And he would wait for a phone call from a pleasant-voiced woman asking him to hold, please, for the president's chief of staff: We need a new national security adviser; or CIA director; or even (now) secretary of state—and the president would like to talk to you.

He was still waiting. There were still people around who could make that call happen. He sometimes did things for those people, and he jealously guarded their good opinion of him. And there were many people around who thought that call might one day come. They sometimes did things for him.

He and his wife had divorced a few years after the Indo-Pakistani War, when it had become clear he was probably never going to be Ambassador Michaelson. Somewhat testily, however, he had rejected the suspicions of Marjorie and others that his marriage had failed *because* of his career-limiting bluntness. Instead he blamed himself. He felt he should have sensed his wife's ebbing confidence, her growing feeling that she was out of place in his world and no longer equal to the demands of a Washington very different from the one she had known in the fifties and sixties. He hadn't. *Surtout, pas assez de zèle.* He knew colleagues who thought the disintegration of his marriage and the yawning ache it produced had deepened him, enhanced the human perspective that informed his dispassionate and often chillingly clinical analyses. He would rather have skipped the pain and taken his chances.

Michaelson had learned about the immediate background to Jim Halliburton's mental illness eighteen months after getting the envelope from Logan. One of the independent counsel (as special prosecutors had come to be called) swarming around Washington at the time had sent a letter to Halliburton in care of Logan, who was representing him. The substance was straightforward: Halliburton was a subject of the investigation; the statute of limitations was about to expire; unless he waived that defense, he would be immediately indicted—which would mean he would have to start paying Logan's hefty legal bills himself instead of passing them on to the Treasury.

"That's what broke him," Logan had told Michaelson with the biting lucidity of calibrated intoxication. "The sniveling little weasels didn't have the guts either to pull the trigger or to lay down the gun. They were just going to leave him hanging. And the people he'd gone out on a limb for stopped returning his calls."

During his career Michaelson had seen women in Iran

publicly flogged for wearing lipstick. He had seen teen-aged boys in Afghanistan strung up by their heels, castrated, and gutted for picking the wrong side in a civil war. But nothing he'd had to look at over three and a half decades of diplomacy had been harder for him than the spectacle of Jim Halliburton during the roughly annual visits Michaelson made to him at the VA Extended Care Facility in Rockville, Maryland. The mind that had mastered Arabic and Hindi was now reduced to incoherent mutterings about briefing Dean Rusk or Cyrus Vance the day before, the once-hard belly left flabby and grotesquely distended by inactivity and pureed food. Eyes that had been coolly analytic were now invaded by feral terror at the mention of standing up. And the thought Michaelson couldn't altogether repress each time he drove away: I have seen the future, and it stinks.

Michaelson had kept Logan's envelope all these years, long after Washington had forgotten Halliburton and whatever affair had enmeshed him, and long after all the independent counsel and congressional investigators had turned in their last expense accounts and folded up shop. He had kept it in adherence to a fundamental Washington principle: Information is currency, and you don't throw some away just because you don't know the denomination. He had also kept it as a pointed reminder, for among the first leaks and hints that had stimulated the investigation that ultimately blasted Halliburton's mind were some disseminated in the line of duty by Richard Michaelson.

Michaelson didn't know much more about the significance of the document inside the envelope now than he had five years before. But he could read. The traveler who had checked out of the St. Demetrius Hotel was Andrew Shepherd. And Imex Tradco had the same street address as Calvert Manor. That, rather than a thoughtful concern for Marjorie Randolph and her friend Patrice Helmsing, was why he had asked her to visit the house with him after Phillips's phone call. And that was why he was going to call on Avery Phillips this afternoon.

Three

Fletcher Park was the name Avery Phillips had given to a northeast Washington, D.C., residential neighborhood after he converted it into a condominium. A discreet private drive led to a secluded parking lot and common area serving eight modest two-story houses. The frame and fieldstone homes were trim and well maintained, with doors of candy-apple red, royal blue, hunter green, and sunshine yellow.

Michaelson found Phillips in a living room heavy on chrome-and-stretched-leather chairs, eggshell carpeting, track lighting, and shelving of lacquered black wood. Phillips, who Michaelson knew was in his early fifties, could easily have passed for his early thirties. You had to concentrate to see the specks of white in his short brown hair. His olive-complected face was smooth—full but without any suggestion of extra chins or sagging jowls.

As Phillips listened to Michaelson's concise analysis of why Calvert Manor couldn't serve his purposes, he sat with his right ankle planted on his left knee, his right shin almost perpendicular to his left thigh. His attitude suggested a kind of coiled relaxation, as if he were a Zen master ready in the next moment to fight, meditate, or make a joke, and not overly concerned about which it would be.

"You're onto something about political fallout," he said, gesturing minimally with a beaded glass of Evian. "But the current asking price would be a stunning bargain for my client, even after renovation costs. I think our friends across the pond will cheerfully absorb a bit of short-term flak. Besides, six percent of two-six is, let's see, carry the three, one hundred fifty-six thousand dollars. Even a slim chance for a commission like that is worth some speculative effort."

"I wouldn't call the chance slim, I'd call it emaciated," Michaelson said. "And even if the EU should decide to go after Calvert Manor, you should know that it's probably going to have to outbid somebody else—which may make the final deal look less like a bargain." Michaelson then explained briefly about Marjorie and Patrice Helmsing.

"You handle political analysis," Phillips said with a tolerant, not-quite-condescending smile. "I'll take care of bidding wars and the formidable Ms. Marjorie Randolph."

A bracing blast of late-winter air announced the opening of Phillips's front door. A bright-eyed young black man wearing a midnight-blue, puffy-sleeved buccaneer shirt and a pair of white leather pants stepped halfway into the room.

"Heads up, Ageless," he said to Phillips in a lilting tenor. "Project's on his way."

"Thank you, Willie," Phillips said, the suggestion of a sigh diluting his voice. He turned an apologetic glance toward Michaelson. "This may become tiresome."

"Don't call him Project, by the way," Willie interjected. "Only his really close friends get away with that."

Michaelson glanced in amused bafflement from Phillips

17

to Willie—Willie Gilchrist, as Michaelson would eventually learn.

"I haven't felt this completely lost since the first interdepartmental meeting I attended my third week as an FSO," he said. "I don't have the faintest idea what you're talking about."

"We do have a penchant for idiom," Phillips said. "Willie regards anyone who can tell a box-and-one from a triangle-two as a basketball fanatic, and he favors us with appropriate nicknames. I'm the Ageless Veteran."

"Ageless for short," explained Willie, who had stepped all the way into the room.

"Project," Phillips continued, "whose mother knows him as Tony Selkirk, is a robust young man who until recently was grabbing rebounds for a locally prominent college squad. Not quite NBA material, as he spent several weeks finding out the hard way."

"David Stern's loss is our gain," Willie chirped.

"With proper planning," Phillips said, "he might catch on in Europe or the Continental Basketball Association next season."

"Why 'Project,' just out of curiosity?" Michaelson asked.

"In basketball," Phillips explained, "a project is a player who has immense physical gifts but who won't be effective without extensive training in court craft and position skills. Willie feels that, at least off the court, Tony belongs in that category."

"A little rough around the edges," Willie confirmed with an emphatic nod. "I must have told him six times that *Private Lives* makes perfectly good sense once you realize that all four characters are really guys. It just doesn't penetrate."

Nodding politely, Michaelson settled back in his chair. He'd delivered the message that was the pretext for his visit, but he had something else he wanted to chat about before he left.

Phillips's postmilitary success in the crowded field of Washington-area real-estate development was a local legend spawning many stories, some not entirely false. Phillips, for example, actually had advertised an Arlington home early in his career as "perfect for rich plumber with a sense of humor." And according to depositions in two lawsuits, he had indeed characterized developing real-estate projects as far simpler than selling houses. "You just take money from doctors and lawyers and spend it more wisely than they would if they were allowed to keep it. Never lie. Fraud suggests an appalling lack of imagination."

With a reputation like that, Michaelson reflected, there must be dozens of people Phillips could have asked to front for him on the Calvert Manor feeler. People far likelier than Michaelson to agree, and who could have performed at least as plausibly. But Phillips had asked Michaelson. And now that Phillips was apparently determined to proceed even though he had to know that the deal he'd described to Michaelson didn't make sense, the next thing Michaelson wanted to know was why.

Project burst into the room less than a minute after Willie's warning. Michaelson thought that he had to be six feet seven inches tall and weigh 230 pounds. A mop of stringy black hair spilled over his forehead. Dark splotches of sweat stained his long-sleeved gray sweatshirt, while muscular legs ruddy with exercise and exposure to cold showed beneath his maroon shorts. He cradled a basketball in his right hand and carried a boom box in his left. Michaelson easily imagined him at a nearby outdoor court, swishing the ball through metal nets to the accompaniment of whatever music people his age listened to these days.

Confusion and alarm played across his candid features

in the few seconds before his eyes glazed over during Phillips's introductions. Nodding briefly at Michaelson, he dumped the basketball and boom box unceremoniously at the door, levered his feet out of his Nikes without completely untying them, and dropped heavily into the chair nearest Phillips. He edged the chair a couple of inches closer to Phillips while Willie gathered the detritus at the door and took it from the room.

"Georgetown is ESPN's first game tonight, so the menu will run to pizza and subs," Phillips said. "Willie should be calling for them any minute. Not up to embassy standards, I know, but you're certainly welcome to stay and share if you'd like."

"I won't impose. I do have a parting question, though."

"Ask."

"Why did you ask me to make the overture for you on Calvert Manor? I'm having a little trouble seeing 'Michaelson' as the first convenient name to pop up on your Rolodex."

"Not the first, to tell you the truth," Phillips said. "There were any number who said no before you did. I'm on the verge of having Willie take a shot, and if he turns me down, the next candidate is my mailman."

"That explains it," Michaelson said, smiling smoothly in polite but total disbelief.

Willie reentered and flipped on a television across the room from the other three.

"Game time already?" Phillips asked, glancing at his watch.

"*Crossfire*," Willie said. "Marcus Humphreys is on up front."

"Ah, good catch," Phillips said, swiveling toward the television. "Turn it up a bit, would you please?"

Willie obeyed in time for the others to hear John Sununu

20

end the preamble to a question with the words "credible presidential candidacy."

"So how about it, Congressman Humphreys," Sununu continued. "When will you drop the coyness and heed the jock-wear slogans 'No Fear/Just Do It'?"

"I think it's more important to do it right than to do it fast," the black congressman whose torso now filled the screen said in measured tones. He still seemed to have all of his salt-and-pepper hair, but his face showed the wear, tear, and character of fifty-seven years. " 'No Fear' doesn't do much for me as a slogan. Acting *despite* fear is brave. Acting *without* fear is dumb."

"Quick with a line, isn't he?" Phillips commented with detached, professional interest. "Doesn't look much like James Earl Jones, though."

"We can't really blame him for that, can we?" Michaelson responded.

Humphreys had been a prosperous physician in Augusta, Georgia, eleven years before when a confrontation with protesters outside an AIDS hospice had propelled him into politics. In *Cold Georgia Rain,* HBO's "fact-based" movie loosely about the incident, James Earl Jones had played Humphreys.

"We can't blame him for any of it," Phillips said. "HBO turned eight tub-thumpers chanting passages from Deuteronomy and Leviticus into a howling mob of three dozen who wanted to burn the hospice down. It converted an anticlimactic demonstration on a cloudy afternoon into a dramatic, late-night siege. And it made Marcus Humphreys into James Earl Jones. The arresting thing is that millions of Americans who saw that HBO movie will swear they were watching live news footage on *Nightline.* What they see on television is more real than reality itself."

"Works for me," Willie said. "Every Jewish guy I know

is funny and every blonde has big tits. Not that I'm paying any attention, of course."

"Well, Marcus Humphreys is a four-term congressman because of it," Phillips said. "And he may well become the first black President of the United States."

"Let's not give HBO all the credit if he does," Michaelson said. "Maybe the demonstrators were just annoying instead of dangerous, and maybe they went away because they'd run out of hymns and it started raining rather than because Doctor Humphreys stood at the door and said Rachel Humphreys would be a widow before they came in. The facts remain that he did stand in front of the door, they didn't come in, and they might have if he hadn't been standing there."

"All of which matters less to me than his position on accelerated depreciation of rental property," Phillips said.

While Michaelson was trying to remember whether that was Phillips's fourth lie of the evening or only his third, *Crossfire*'s camera switched to Sununu and a liberal du jour preparing to talk at each other. Rising from his chair and crossing the room, Phillips dimmed the lights and switched channels on the television.

As soon as the thudding, familiar basketball action flickered onto the screen, Phillips muted the volume. He put a CD into a player and stroked it on. In moments the strains of Mozart's Piano Concerto No. 21 washed through the room, providing an eerily appropriate counterpoint to the alternately violent and balletic basketball game.

"Thank you for your hospitality," Michaelson said as he got up. He found the idea of watching basketball played to Mozart oddly appealing, but he sensed unmistakably that at this point the room was overcrowded by one.

Four

C an I offer you some breakfast?" Catherine Shepherd asked as she plucked a halved bagel from the toaster.

"Thanks, but I've already eaten," said Marjorie, who like most people who work for a living usually took care of her morning meal well before nine-fifteen.

It was two days after Marjorie's first visit to Calvert Manor. Marjorie had gotten Michaelson's report on his conversation with Phillips and Patrice Helmsing's reaction to her own description of the home. She had concluded that serious negotiations had to be started immediately and conducted with finesse. The first name that came to mind for the job was hers. So here she was with her legs under the kitchen table at Calvert Manor.

After dabbing the bagel halves with margarine, Catherine laid them next to a slice of cantaloupe on a blue china plate. She then put the plate over a linen serviette on the butcher-block table in the kitchen's sunniest corner, where Marjorie was already sitting. Seating herself, Catherine poured grapefruit juice into two tumblers and with a gesture invited Marjorie to take one.

"Your friend's a real possibility, then?" she asked.

"Patrice Helmsing has her own accounts with two stockbrokers," Marjorie said. "Her most recent husband has an acute desire to delight her. She wants to come back to the Washington area, and she's interested enough in Calvert Manor that she'd like to fly in from Detroit this week to see the place."

"Will Friday afternoon work?" Catherine asked after swallowing a morsel of bagel.

"Should. I'll check and get back to you by Thursday to confirm it."

"We really could have done this over the phone, couldn't we?" Catherine mused. "Why did you drive all the way out here just to set up an appointment?"

Marjorie stalled for a moment with a sip of grapefruit juice. She had no objection in principle to telling the truth, but she felt you had to know when to stop.

"I think there's going to be at least one other potential buyer in the picture," she said. "Of course, that may just mean that it comes down to who bids more, which will make everything rather simple. But I hope it doesn't, and I came out here so I could tell you why, face-to-face."

"Please do," Catherine said.

"The other buyer is an agent acting for the European Union. He supposedly wants to buy Calvert Manor so the EU can turn it into its U.S. trade office."

"I can't say that I'm very enthusiastic about that idea," Catherine said. "Although I suppose it's naïve of me to admit it."

"That's the instinct I'm counting on," Marjorie said. "When you were explaining so carefully why it made sense to sell the house, I got the feeling that Calvert Manor wasn't just a showplace that your father bought to impress customers—that for you it really was a home. If you don't mind it becoming an office for bureaucrats instead of a home for someone else, that's up to you. But I felt you ought to have the choice openly presented to you."

"I didn't really appreciate what Calvert Manor meant for Dad when I was a girl," Catherine said with an understanding nod. "Looking back on it, I think he saw this place as something solid and real. Those big international deals he put together paid the bills, but to him there wasn't all that much substance to them."

"They must have had some substance if they paid the kind of bills a place like this would run up," Marjorie said.

Catherine shook her head with a half smile.

"Dad used to say that in the early seventies the only way an American with an MBA and a Slavic language could avoid making money was to enter a Trappist monastery. That was the heyday of détente. Peace in the world through Pepsi in Moscow. He thought that doing those deals really was changing things. Then, as Dad put it, an old man dies in Portugal, Cubans start fighting in Africa, and it all goes blooey overnight. He kept on making money, but now that was all he was doing. Calvert Manor was something that wouldn't just go up in smoke like the détente stuff."

"This may sound opportunistic," Marjorie said, "but that's the same kind of meaning this place would have for Patrice Helmsing. Patrice is black and she's been a special friend of mine since college. Even when we haven't seen each other for two or three years, Patrice and I can sit around a fire with cabernet and crudités for hours, talking about Washington in the 1960s and London in the 1790s and our first husbands and last children and everything in between. Her roots are in Washington, and a place like this would have an extraordinary resonance for her."

Marjorie thought she'd overdone it, and she expected

Catherine to glance away. She didn't. Instead, Catherine opened her eyes wide and gazed straight at Marjorie with a countenance suggesting the most inexpressible longing Marjorie had ever seen. She looked like a ragged kid from the slums hearing a description of some lushly Arcadian summer camp.

"That sounds so lovely," she said in a voice between a whisper and a sob.

In Catherine Shepherd's eyes at that moment Marjorie saw exquisite loneliness. For an instant, Marjorie imagined herself suggesting impulsively that she and Catherine just blow off the day, blitz Woodies, have bacon cheeseburgers and chocolate malts someplace where they'd need the National Debt Clock to count the calories, cruise through the Corcoran Gallery, stop for cocktails at Clyde's, and straggle back to Calvert Manor at twilight with armloads of parcels and a little edge-off-the-day buzz. For a long time afterward, reflecting on their chat in the kitchen nook striped by the cold winter sun, Marjorie wondered if everything might have turned out differently had she acted on that impulse. But she didn't. The moment passed.

"I think you're right about the European Union thing, by the way," Catherine said suddenly in a more business-like voice, giving her head a little forget-that-last-part flick. "Wilcox called to say that an inquiry had come from someone whose name I can't remember."

"Avery Phillips?" Marjorie suggested.

"Not sure. Wilcox said the guy was some kind of high-powered dealer-developer, and she suspected he was representing an undisclosed principal. This place hasn't pulled a nibble in weeks, so I'm betting the call to Wilcox is from the same alternative buyer you've been talking about."

"Safe bet," Marjorie said.

Catherine's last sip of grapefruit juice left a sixteenth-inch of pulp and liquid in the bottom of the glass. She put her knife and fork together on her plate in the four o'clock position. Then three quick thumps on the back stairway gave Catherine and Marjorie a second or two warning before Cindy burst into the kitchen.

"Oh," Cindy said, gaping at Marjorie, "you're back."

"That's Cindy's way of saying, 'Excuse me for interrupting,' " Catherine said.

"I swear to God, Cathy," Cindy said, shaking her head at the place setting, "if Martha Stewart ever needs an enema, she's going to have you hold the tube."

Cindy was wearing a bright pink T-shirt with the words PRETTY GIRLS SMOKING CIGARETTES circling a silhouette depicting approximately that. Her denim shorts showed ten inches of thigh below ragged hems and a generous smidgeon of cheek through a hole near the left rear pocket. She was carrying an enormous book covered with what looked like very old, very thick paper hand-folded into a dust jacket. Marjorie wondered if Danielle Steel had produced a bildungsroman that *Publisher's Weekly* had somehow missed. Then she realized with astonishment that it was a Bible.

"Good morning," Catherine said.

"Mmff," Cindy said as she bent into the refrigerator.

More steps echoing on the stairway answered her. A man in his early twenties lurched into the kitchen. He was wearing white painter's pants and a T-shirt identical to Cindy's. As he took in the tableau before him, he shook his head with enough enthusiasm to produce a faint tinkle from thirteen small gold rings bunched along the top of his left ear and the outside of his left nostril.

"Miss Randolph," Catherine said, "this is C-Sharp. C-Sharp, Marjorie Randolph."

"Delighted," Marjorie said.

"Looks like snow outside," C-Sharp mumbled after a barely perceptible nod.

"I hate Washington when it snows," Cindy said with reflexive vehemence that seemed disproportionate to the topic. "Washington's just ridiculous about snow."

" 'Pretty Girls Smoking Cigarettes' is a song, by the way," Catherine explained to Marjorie as she noticed her examining the T-shirts. "C-Sharp expects it to be his group's breakthrough hit."

"Fuckin' right," C-Sharp said.

Cindy emerged from the refrigerator with a can of Diet Coke and three slices of pizza piled high with congealed mozzarella and clumsily wrapped in aluminum foil. She offered some to C-Sharp, who blinked and looked like he'd need to think about it.

"Where'd you dig the Bible up?" Catherine asked bemusedly.

"I've been looking for readings for you to use when you and Preston make it legal."

"How thoughtful," Catherine said, the way Miss Manners might have.

"Okay, be an asshole, but I've found one. Listen."

Opening the Bible on the counter, Cindy took a deep breath, shook hair out of her eyes, and began reading in a slow cadence with a voice as close to a TV evangelist's as an alto could manage.

"A reading from the Book of Numbers, chapter thirty-one. 'They made war on Midian, as Yahweh had ordered Moses, and put every male to death. The Israelites took the Midianite women and their little ones captive and carried off all their cattle, all their flocks and all their goods as booty. Moses was enraged with the officers of the army who had come back from this expedition. He said, "Why have you spared the life of all the women? Kill all the male children and kill all the women who have ever slept with a man; but spare the lives of the young girls who have never slept with a man, and keep them for yourselves.' "

Cindy waited long enough after she glanced up from the scriptural account to let the silence—slightly open-mouthed, in Catherine's case—hang a bit heavy.

"Don't you like it?" she asked then, feigning a hurt look. "I think it's a very moving tribute to the virtues of virginity."

Wet, heavy snow began to fall shortly after Marjorie left Calvert Manor. It fell fast and hard, in soggy, smacking clumps that the wipers fought to clear from her windshield. By the time she came within hoping distance of Connecticut Avenue, she realized this was serious stuff—a long, traffic-mangling storm.

Which left Marjorie with time to wonder why in the world Cindy would have gone to such an immense amount of trouble, plowing through what must have been the thoroughly unfamiliar pages of the Old Testament, to come up with a lame, one-shot joke. It wasn't until she finally pulled into a snow-swept parking space two hundred yards from Cavalier Books that an intuitively plausible if not logically supportable answer occurred to her.

"I wonder if Preston Demarest is Jewish?" she said to herself.

Five

If Cecilia Hamisch had behaved like a normal, self-respecting civil servant, Michaelson reflected at ten o'clock the next morning, he'd be sitting in his office reviewing an earnest research paper instead of standing in the snow committing a felony. Or maybe only a misdemeanor, but even so.

Yesterday's snow, falling thick and heavy well into the night, gave federal employees an ironclad excuse to goldbrick. As he walked from his Georgetown apartment down a surreally underpopulated Massachusetts Avenue to his office, Michaelson assumed that none of the former State Department colleagues he planned to call would be in. He would leave messages explaining what he wanted. This would pin him to his desk for the rest of the morning, on the off chance that one of them would wander in by ten and get back to him before lunch. By adopting this tactic he would force himself to pass several character-building hours reviewing a Brookings Junior Fellow's analysis of the proposed common European currency, which this week was being called the euro.

Cecilia Hamisch upset this carefully scripted scenario by being diligently at her desk when Michaelson called at nine-ten. Hamisch was a midlevel Foreign Service officer whose lengthy title included the terms "liaison" and "World Trade Organization." This meant that her actual function was to remind the Office of the United States Trade Representative that trade policy was a component of foreign policy rather than the other way around.

She had worked under Michaelson for a couple of years before his retirement from the State Department. Given the vagaries of political fortune, it wasn't impossible that she'd find herself working for him again someday. So he was gratified but not surprised when she promised to call him at four P.M. with a report on whatever she'd found out.

This meant that Michaelson no longer had anything chaining him to his phone for the next several hours. He dug the latest draft of the euro paper out of his box only long enough to decorate its cover page with an oversized Post-it on which he printed neatly in black, felt-tip pen:

> Your evidence and analysis seem to prove incontrovertibly that the euro is both inevitable and impossible. Is it wise to rely on the dynamic tension between these possibilities, or do you propose to choose one or the other? Let's discuss. RM

With that, he consigned the euro paper to his out box and pulled a metropolitan phone directory from the back of his credenza. It took him ten seconds to look up Demarest, Preston R. Demarest's phone rang fifteen times without either an answer or the intervention of a recorded invitation to leave a message. Such technological self-denial seemed anomalous to Michaelson, who would have given even odds that Demarest took his pager into the shower and had a fax machine in his car.

Objectively, that merited no more than a shrug and a mental note. Subjectively, however, Michaelson had a sharper taste for concrete problems than for theoretical woolgathering. The concrete problems at the moment were that he didn't know what Avery Phillips was up to—whatever it was seemed to involve both Michaelson and Jim Halliburton—and for reasons that went well beyond idle curiosity Michaelson therefore wanted to find out what was actually on Phillips's agenda. The address shown for Demarest was within manageable walking distance of the Alexandria Metro stop. Michaelson grabbed his battered topcoat and tweed walking hat and headed for the door.

The address turned out to be the lower flat in a two-story house that had been divided into an upstairs and a downstairs apartment. The first thing Michaelson noticed was the mail overflowing the box beside the door. It certainly hadn't been delivered this morning, which suggested that Demarest hadn't been home since at least yesterday. Michaelson concluded that he was ringing the doorbell strictly for the exercise, and he was right.

It was at that point, as he started going through Demarest's mail, that he began wondering how serious a crime he was committing—and grumbling mentally that there was never a lawyer sitting around on someone's front porch when you needed one.

Demarest's mail started with bills and *Newsweek*. Then came a letter of some kind from a health club in the district called Bodies by Design; a fund-raising appeal from a group that wished to fight censorship in public schools; and a letter from the District of Columbia Corporations

Commission, addressed to Club Chat Fouette, in care of Demarest.

Michaelson was considering whether the absence of an *accent aigu* from the last item meant anything when a measured voice cutting sharply through the cold air commanded his attention.

"What are you doing there?"

Turning his head unhurriedly to the right in reaction to this challenge, Michaelson saw a woman with rust-tinged gray hair which at the moment was less than kempt. She wore a blue terry cloth robe over pink pajamas and unbuckled galoshes. She was holding her right hand behind her back. Michaelson suspected that the hand gripped a gun. Handgun ownership is widespread in Virginia, and residents of that state's Washington suburbs assume that any interloper from the district arrives with felonious intent.

"I'm looking for Mr. Demarest," Michaelson said affably behind a harmless-codger smile. "I have something for him."

"He's not home. Whatever it is, you can leave it with me."

"I wouldn't dream of burdening you with it," Michaelson said as he casually replaced Demarest's mail. "I was considering leaving it in his mailbox, but on reflection I'm afraid I don't feel comfortable with that option. He doesn't seem to collect his mail very regularly, and in any event we must respect the sanctity of the post. You don't know when he'll be home, do you?"

"I'd call that his business. Who would you be, exactly?"

"My name is Richard Michaelson. I have a card here."

"Skip it," she said as he began to reach for his card case.

Michaelson complied with a complacent shrug.

"I would appreciate it very much if you'd tell him I dropped by and am looking forward to his call," he said.

"I'll tell him you trooped over here and rifled his mail."

"I hope he realizes how fortunate he is to have such a vigilant landlady," Michaelson said, laying it on a bit thick as he prepared to offer his back to a woman he was now absolutely convinced was armed and tightly wound.

"I'm not his landlady," the woman said. "I'm his tenant."

"In that case he's even luckier than I thought. Good day."

Touching the brim of his cap and smiling as if he were auditioning for the kind of role David Niven used to get, Michaelson turned from the woman and began walking away. He didn't risk self-congratulation until he'd made it to the Metro stop without catching a bullet between his shoulder blades.

Potomac Telephone had long since given up chaining phone books to pay phones, but Club Chat Fouetté turned up, acute accent in place, in a weekend entertainment guide at a news box in the Metro station. The ad gave an address on New York Avenue, about four blocks from Bodies by Design, so Michaelson took the subway all the way to Federal Triangle instead of getting off at Foggy Bottom.

The place struck Michaelson as about two steps up the scale from the standard New York Avenue establishment. More typical of the neighborhood were the shop across the street advertising XXX VIDEO PRIVATE BOOTHS and a place with opaque windows four doors down that slyly promised WOMEN'S CLOTHES 90% OFF. Club Chat Fouetté's vermillion facade wasn't exactly a model of understatement, but the neon guitar decorating its window and its offer of "Live Music Nitely" seemed quaintly sedate by comparison to the rest of the block.

No one responded to Michaelson's rap on the locked front door. The alley led to a side door with a buzzer, which he pushed. A thirty-second wait was rewarded with a lock snapping inside the door followed by a four-inch crack between the door and its frame.

"No delivery before noon, that the deal," a male voice with a vaguely Slavic tincture said through the crack.

"No delivery, I need to talk to Mr. Demarest."

"Can't help you," the voice said.

"You can, actually," Michaelson said. "He does work here, you know. He gets official mail for the place, and he belongs to a health club within walking distance. If he's in at the moment, why don't you ask him if he'd like to chat with Richard Michaelson?"

"Can't help you," the voice repeated.

Michaelson had already braced himself to have the door slammed in his face when he heard an indistinct shout from deeper in the building. The Slavic voice yelled an approximation of "Michaelson" in response. Whatever came back must have been affirmative because the door opened wider. Michaelson went in.

The man who admitted him was slightly built, perhaps five-seven with a surprisingly fair complexion set off by black hair that seemed lacquered to his scalp. He wore Levis, Doc Martens, and an open-necked man's button-down dress shirt over an olive drab T-shirt, as if undecided about whether to dress like a lumberjack or a lawyer on casual day.

Following him, Michaelson stepped into a surprisingly elegant saloon. Banquettes of plum-colored stuff that could pass for leather in the dim light lined the far wall. Taking up most of the floor were chairs with backs and arms of oxblood velveteen plush surrounding black tabletops as shiny as any floor Fred and Ginger ever waltzed on. The bar was white, making it look longer than it was. A mauve baby grand took up almost all of a tiny stage.

Demarest waited at the bottom of a stairway just beyond

the stage. A buff-colored vest covered most of the pea-green tie knotted over his deep copper shirt. He was holding a green sport coat casually over his left shoulder. Once Michaelson had had five seconds to absorb the full impact of his ensemble, Demarest slipped the sport coat on.

"What is it you have for me?" he asked.

"Questions and advice."

"I'm not in the market for either. But come on up anyway."

Demarest effected an effortless pivot and briskly mounted the stairs. Michaelson circled the stage and by hustling a bit managed to reach the mezzanine at the top of the stairs in time to see Demarest step behind a shoulder-high partition in the most distant corner. When Michaelson reached the partition he saw Demarest standing at a scarred wooden desk, pouring chardonnay into a Styrofoam cup beside a twelve-function telephone console.

"Some for you?" Demarest asked.

"Not this early, thank you. Water will be fine."

"Can do." He filled a second cup with LaCroix water and put it in front of Michaelson. Then he raised his own drink.

"It's definitely not too early in England," he said, and took a generous swallow. "Which first, questions or advice?"

"I'd like to know how you met Catherine Shepherd."

"Why?"

"Do you know who Jim Halliburton is?"

"Never heard of him," Demarest said.

"He was a colleague of mine who once upon a time sent me a message. Avery Phillips was also once a colleague of mine, and he recently asked me a favor. The message Halliburton sent and the favor Phillips asked have Calvert Manor in common. The first and last time I saw the place you were the only non-Shepherd there, ostensibly because

36

you know Catherine Shepherd. You two don't strike me as people who travel regularly in the same circles. That's why."

Demarest smiled complacently and sipped some more wine.

"I don't think you have a clue about the circles I travel in," he murmured. "All you know is that I live in Alexandria and I'm the registered agent for a niche market nightspot."

"On the contrary, I have far more information about you than I can properly digest," Michaelson said. "I've already mentioned that you belong to a health club within walking distance of this nightspot but a long way from your home. Conclusion: You're not just a registered agent for this place; you spend a good deal of time here on a regular basis. You take telephone messages here and not at your apartment. The woman who lives above you was alarmed but not surprised when a strange man appeared at your residence asking impertinent questions—indicating that today wasn't the first time that had happened. She thought my asking after you was important enough to inform you about it immediately, because otherwise you wouldn't have had any reason to believe I had something for you. Now, perhaps you and Ms. Shepherd met while discussing NAFTA and single malt scotch during intermission at a Kennedy Center chamber music concert, but I'm betting the other way."

"You're extrapolating rather aggressively from minimal data."

"In the Foreign Service that was roughly half my job."

"I hope you did the other half better," Demarest said. "You'll be embarrassed at how badly astray you've led yourself. Catherine and I met through the Stuart Restoration Society."

"Which is what?" Michaelson asked.

"A small group dedicated to restoring the Stuart dynasty to the English throne. We believe that James the Second was the last legitimate English monarch, that the grotesquely misnamed Glorious Revolution in 1688 was an unprincipled usurpation, and that the churlish balls-ups achieved by the current so-called royals are exactly what you should expect from a bunch of horse-faced German interlopers—which is what they happen to be."

"I can see where a project like that could turn into a full-time job," Michaelson said dryly.

"Our efforts in support of the cause so far have been discreet and restrained. We gather occasionally to cheer against the College of William and Mary if it's involved in an athletic contest that anyone cares about. We send press releases to *Majesty* magazine. We maintain a Web site. We sell men's ties with the Stuart crest. We talk endlessly about organizing a tourist boycott of England until the rightful heir—happens to be a woman, and we have her identified—is recognized."

"Very ambitious."

"And, of course," Demarest concluded, "we hold a high tea on Restoration Day—the anniversary of Charles the Second resuming the throne. That specifically is how I met Catherine."

"While she was discussing the Bloody Assizes with Judge Jeffreys over Earl Grey and scones?"

"Not exactly," Demarest said after a long moment's silence. Shifting his eyes abruptly from Michaelson, he stared into the middle distance, as if he were lining up a six-iron shot. "I approached her about permission to use Calvert Manor for the Restoration Day tea. The place dates from the time of James the Second, you know. She had never heard of us, but the idea charmed her right out of her navy blue flats. Her concentration at Bucknell was the literature and history of seventeenth-century England.

She's an SRS natural. The rest is basically *Love Story* without the leukemia and foul language."

"How long ago was this first charmed encounter?"

"Roughly thirty seconds before Cindy started hating my guts."

"I was thinking more in terms of months or years."

"Tell me something," Demarest said, suddenly resuming eye contact with Michaelson. "What in the world does that have to do with whatever it is about these Halliburton and Phillips guys that has you bothered?"

"If your offer is still good," Michaelson said instead of answering the question, "I'll take you up on some of that wine."

"Sure," Demarest said.

He quickly produced another Styrofoam cup and decanted chardonnay into it. Michaelson lifted his cup six inches off the desk, caught Demarest's eye, and then said with almost liturgical solemnity, "To the queen." He passed his wine cup deliberately above the top of the water cup and waited expectantly. Demarest again looked blank for a second or two.

"To the queen," he stammered then.

"The answer to your question," Michaelson said, "is that I don't know what the timing of your first meeting with Catherine Shepherd has to do with what I'm looking into. If anything. I do know, however, that the Stuart Restoration Society is an elaborate cover story, suggesting that you're a bit sensitive about how your two paths actually crossed."

"The Stuart Restoration Society is perfectly genuine," Demarest said. "You can check it out."

"I'm certain it is. I'm equally certain that no one deeply involved in such a group would be baffled by an allusion to Judge Jeffreys and the Bloody Assizes, when the streets ran red with gore from unfortunates who had rebelled prematurely against the Stuart monarchy. A true Stuart partisan would condemn the very term 'Bloody Assizes' as Whig propaganda."

"I was trying to be diplomatic," Demarest said.

"And what were you trying to be when I offered the classic toast of Stuart loyalists?" Michaelson asked. "After the Stuarts went into exile, their supporters in England always had both wine and water at dinner. When someone toasted King William or his successors, they'd join in, to avoid appearing disloyal. But they'd pass their wineglass above their water glass so that their toast would actually be 'To the king over the water'—in other words, to the exiled pretender. I have a quite emphatic impression that you didn't know a thing about that until this moment."

"It's a bit esoteric," Demarest said.

"Translation: It wasn't in your briefing book."

"This conversation is beginning to bore me," Demarest said.

One of the most underappreciated weapons in a diplomat's arsenal is the simple truth, brutally stated. As Demarest pulled a black-and-orange vinyl carrying bag onto the desktop and began checking impatiently through it, Michaelson decided to use that weapon.

"You're in over your head," he said, not unkindly.

"Thank you for sharing."

"You're not in Avery Phillips's league. Few people are. You're not going to scam him and you're not going to outwit him."

"I hadn't even heard his name until you mentioned it a few minutes ago," Demarest said as he zipped the gym bag shut.

"You don't have to admit anything. Just absorb what I'm saying and think about it. If you think you're using him, the chances are that he's using you. If you double-cross him, you're in trouble, and if you play along with him, you're out in the cold as soon as he's gotten what he wants from you."

Demarest made sure all the desk drawers were locked, then offered Michaelson a tight little smile.

"Anything else?" he asked.

"Of course," Michaelson said. "Tell me what's actually going on. I'm not looking for money or a piece of the action. I just want to know the story behind a piece of paper that I got from someone I worked with long ago. What's in it for you is that with the help I can give you you might stand a chance against Phillips."

"Have a good life," Demarest said, turning the smile off. He strode quickly away, toward the stairs.

After Demarest's head disappeared beneath the top of the stairwell, Michaelson took a handbill from the desk. It advertised a return engagement the following week for "C-Sharp and the Nasty Boys."

Michaelson waited ten minutes before he walked to the squat, chrome-and-glass office building whose fourth floor sheltered Bodies by Design. He went there to see if the gym bag Demarest had been flashing around was a red herring or if he actually had just gone to the place.

He had. In the midst of a sales pitch from a husky young man who looked like he had a pulse rate of about sixty, Michaelson spotted Demarest cruising around the oval running track, swiveling his head for a long, appreciative gaze each time he passed the aerobics area. And when the aerobics class ended and the swivel gazes continued, Michaelson surmised that Demarest had been ogling neither the men nor the women in their formfitting spandex, but the mirror.

"Patrice Helmsing is confirmed for three o'clock tomorrow afternoon," Marjorie told Catherine Shepherd an hour or so later.

"Well, that's good news. I'll let Wilcox know. Cindy and I will both be here. And of course you're welcome to come if you can take the time from your store. This is really your party."

"I probably will stop by," Marjorie said. "With the snow we've only had three customers today, and unless there's a sudden thaw, I don't expect tomorrow to be any better. Have you had any luck getting a plowing service out there for the driveway?"

"No," Catherine said, "they're all swamped. And I guess it could be a problem, couldn't it?"

"Your driveway does dip a bit in the middle. If it's acting like a bobsled run tomorrow afternoon, you may end up with an alienated prospect and a brace of unexpected weekend houseguests."

"Well, Cindy and I will just have to take care of it ourselves, that's all."

"That sounds a bit ambitious," Marjorie said. Delicately. At least in Cindy's case, any commitment to manual labor struck Marjorie as insanely implausible.

"Thank you for expressing your skepticism so tactfully," Catherine said, a suggestion of joshing laughter coloring her voice. "Cindy already brought the idea up, actually. She said she's so anxious to unload this place that she'd do anything except change diapers. Not a job for princesses, I grant you, but Cindy and I between us should be able to handle it. We've agreed we'll be out here in our grubs by noon tomorrow if we haven't arranged for commercial plowing by then."

"Good luck, then," Marjorie said. Catherine sounded confident, but Marjorie would believe it when she saw it.

"Sorry it took so long to get back to you," Cecilia Hamisch said over the phone to Michaelson at exactly four o'clock. "The European Union's not at the top of anyone's list right now. But I finally got some calls returned and I have an answer for you."

"Which is what?" Michaelson asked.

"Someone's kidding you. The EU has options on about eighty thousand square feet in downtown Washington. They got a couple of hints from us early on about available space. They were thinking very low profile—handful of secretaries, a few number crunchers, and a face-man to pat fannies over at Commerce. They're definitely not in the market for anything like Calvert Manor."

"So they say, at any rate," Michaelson offered.

"They're putting their money where their mouth is. Those options didn't come cheap."

This was easier than the *New York Times* Monday crossword, Michaelson reflected, with some misgivings. Why would Avery Phillips bother with a phony story that he had to know Michaelson could explode with a phone call or two?

"Thank you very much," Michaelson said.

"There's one more thing," Hamisch said. "My E-mail inquiry stimulated wider interest than I expected. Someone named Connaught called me from one of the national committee offices. Alumnus. I don't remember him, but he seemed to know you and a lot of other people who've worked here. He didn't know anything about the European Union, but he wanted to learn everything I could tell him about Calvert Manor. Which wasn't much."

"That's interesting," Michaelson said. "Thank you."

After hanging up Michaelson pulled an old copy of the studbook off a bookshelf behind him. This was the Foreign Service Personnel Directory, with a capsule biography of all serving FSOs. Connaught, Corbin (James), AB (History) Brown 1965, was credited with service as an attaché for cultural affairs in Belgrade from 1969 to 1974, a science and technology attaché in Prague from 1979 to 1981, and a chargé d'affaires for special assignments in Budapest from 1987 to 1990. No indication of how he'd passed his time during the rather noticeable gaps between these tours of duty.

In other words, Corbin James Connaught was a spook. Or had been. A CIA officer who sometimes used State Department cover. Now ostensibly no longer in government service but claiming to earn his shekels working for one of the political parties. Cecilia Hamisch, model civil servant that she was, had been careful not to say which one.

Michaelson felt a bit silly now about lecturing Demarest on his naïveté. Phillips's fairy tale about the European Union made no sense as a story to fool Michaelson for long. It made very good sense, however, as a device to send a signal with Richard Michaelson's credibility behind it to Washington's foreign policy, national security, and political establishments. A signal that somebody had an interest in Calvert Manor that they were trying to disguise. Which was exactly what Michaelson had just done.

Six

T his is above and beyond, Marjorie," Patrice Helmsing said as the airport retreated in Marjorie's rear-
view mirror late Friday morning. "You're running
a bookstore, not a taxi service."

"I told Carrie to close the store at noon, actually," Marjorie said. "If this morning's sales cover the light bill, I'll
be pleasantly surprised. Snow they shrug off overnight in
Detroit or Chicago paralyzes D.C. for a week."

"That does ring a bell," Helmsing said, smiling slightly.

Patrice Murchison Armour Helmsing was almost six feet
tall. Her white skirt-and-jacket suit and the gold rims of
her glasses stood out strikingly against her obsidian skin.
Gentle waves of hair blacker than her body framed prominent cheekbones that kept her fifties-plus face from seeming fleshy. Eyes with charcoal-flecked, chocolate brown
pupils took in the world with a steady, measured gaze.

Helmsing had lived away from Washington for twenty
of the last twenty-five years, but she still referred to her
family as "the Washington Murchisons." Black Murchi-

sons were free residents of Washington, D.C., ten years before South Carolina fired on Fort Sumter. A generation later they were financially comfortable, and by the 1920s they were rich—part of a class as self-conscious as any collection of blue bloods in Boston or New York. They ran charities, sat on civic committees, funded scholarships, decorated corporate boards, and spent money and sweat battling for civil rights.

A mantle of clouds turned the sky eggshell white from one horizon to the other as Marjorie and Helmsing crawled through half-plowed streets toward Calvert Manor. It was nearly three P.M. when they parked just outside the eight-foot evergreen hedge shielding the property. As soon as they reached the top of the driveway, they spotted a solitary, parka-bundled figure thirty feet away, vigorously attacking the asphalt with an ice chopper.

"Which Shepherd is that?" Helmsing asked.

"Catherine, I'm guessing," Marjorie said.

"Goddammit! Break, you miserable sonofabitch!" the figure barked at the ice.

"Correction," Marjorie said to Helmsing. "Cindy."

Five steps father down the driveway Marjorie raised her voice so that Cindy could hear it over the ice chopper's tinny ring.

"Where's Catherine?"

"Her serene highness stood me up," Cindy panted. "About half an hour ago she breezed back here from someplace where people's shoes match their purses."

"Where is she now?"

"Inside. She was properly mortified and pathetically keen to pitch in, but I told her that perspiration wouldn't coordinate well with the Laura Ashley Junior League Collection getup she had on. I sent her into the house to make herself useful there."

Sweat pasted Cindy's hair to her forehead. A deep red

suffused her face. Marjorie repented her mental disparagement of Cindy's aptitude for hard work and was searching for some gracious way to say so when an inch-thick slab of ice the size of Marjorie's back broke free. Spidery fissures snaked through the remaining layer. Cindy attacked these with atavistic avidity, quickly exposing another twelve square feet of asphalt.

A Lexus pulled into the driveway.

"Wilcox and Jenkins," Cindy said. "Trustee and realtor."

When the two women who got out of the Lexus had made their way down the driveway, Cindy managed perfunctory introductions and offered distracted contributions to a bit of small talk, all punctuated by clanging blows of the chopper blade.

"This is a magnificent piece of work you've done on the driveway," Jenkins said to Cindy, who had by now produced clear pavement to just past the front walk.

"Right," Cindy muttered as she shouldered the snow shovel and ice chopper and started down the driveway toward the garage behind the house. "Now you do a magnificent job of moving this pile of prerevolutionary brick. Then we'll both be happy."

Using Wilcox's key, the four remaining women proceeded into the house without waiting for Cindy to return. They found the large living-room hearth glowing with a bright-flamed fire of crackling cherry wood. They saw fresh apples, oranges, and peaches heaped in a bowl on the dining-room table. Curtains parted on the south side of the house emphasized the cheering effect of the day's scant sunshine. Marjorie surmised that Catherine had been efficiently busy since Cindy had sent her inside.

Which was fine, Marjorie thought, but where was Catherine now? Moping with remorse or not, letting four people walk into her home without even a greeting didn't seem like her style. So far, all they had was Cindy's word about Catherine's whereabouts today. A tiny bite of anxiety began to gnaw at Marjorie's gut.

She told herself she was being silly. Even so, she thought, it couldn't hurt to keep her eyes open.

"The inside looks fabulous too," Jenkins said. "They may start wondering why they need me."

"Just persuade Ms. Helmsing to offer us a price that a court will approve if one of the little darlings decides two years from now to charge me with misfeasance," Wilcox said. "As long as I can turn in a final accounting that's pluperfect bullet proof, you won't have to worry about what the Misses Shepherd think."

Taking the unsubtle hint, Jenkins clicked into sales mode. She adopted a prudently understated approach, letting the home speak for itself. It had plenty to say: colonial heritage, large bedrooms with individual fireplaces, library with oak shelving graced by calf-bound estate books dating to the eighteenth century, ample closet space, and modern plumbing and appliances.

The undeniable downsides of a house more than three centuries old seemed pale in comparison to these features. Some of the renovations the home had seen over the years had been jury-rigged improvisations, resulting in anomalies like doors that opened out of converted bathrooms instead of into them. The door connecting one of the guest bedrooms to its bathroom had a sixty-year-old dead bolt snap lock that would have been more appropriate on an outside back door. When they got to that room, Helmsing seemed instinctively to suspect the weakness in the bolt's spring and the play in its housing, which she promptly verified.

But Marjorie figured things that a few thousand dollars and a little love could fix weren't going to keep Helmsing from owning this house. During the tour of the first and second floors, Helmsing looked like a very serious potential buyer. While Marjorie made discreet forays into empty rooms in a vain search for Catherine, Helmsing turned on taps, flushed toilets, and felt for drafts at the cracks of window frames. When in the midst of viewing what had been the master bedroom she started taking measurements with a cased, metal tape, Marjorie thought the earnest-money check was as good as written.

"If you'll be here for a while yet, I'm going to excuse myself for a few minutes," Marjorie said.

Jenkins nodded while Helmsing scratched numbers in a small memo book. After exiting, Marjorie opened and closed the nearest bathroom door but didn't go inside. She scurried instead toward the stairs. She'd had at least a peek at every room on two floors without spotting Catherine. The glimpse of lonely desperation she'd seen in Catherine's eyes across her kitchen table slipped into Marjorie's memory and wouldn't go away.

After a rapid and fruitless repeat run through the first floor, Marjorie took the kitchen stairs to the basement.

"Catherine?" she called at the bottom of the stairs. Only the faintly mocking echo of her own voice answered her.

Flipping on lights, she moved quickly through the musty cellar. The laundry room was spotless and uninhabited. The furnace room was piled high with empty boxes but showed no sign of recent human intrusion.

She stepped from the furnace room into a spacious recreation room, paneled and carpeted and dominated by a massive pool table. Arrayed haphazardly on shelves around the room's perimeter were the remnants of affluent childhood: board games in battered boxes, Ping-Pong paddles and discolored balls, odd lots of checkers, and the kind of educational books that are received at Christmas without being asked for and shelved by spring without being read.

One last door presented itself to Marjorie. What might have been a small office or an oversized closet intruded into the far corner of the rec room. Cindy leaned against the wall next to the door, paging idly through a copy of *Entertainment Weekly.*

"Where's Catherine?" Marjorie asked.

"Where she wants to be."

"I was looking for more specific information."

"It's not your day to watch her," Cindy said. She snapped the magazine shut. "Don't worry about it. She's a big girl."

"Do you mind if I take a look behind that door?"

"Yes, I mind."

"I just want to be sure Catherine's all right," Marjorie said.

"If there was anything wrong with her, do you think I'd be standing here like an airhead? She's my sister."

"And coheir."

"What's that supposed to mean?"

"It means I'd like to take a look behind that door."

"Listen. Carefully. Catherine and I are both grown-ups. As in of age. Adults. The answer's no. No one's bought anything yet. This is still our house. You go find your little friends and start collaborating on an article for *Gracious Living.*"

"The group upstairs includes a realtor with keys and a trustee with authority," Marjorie said. "Whatever's on the other side of that door, would you rather all four of us saw it or just me?"

"Jesus, you *are* a bitch, aren't you?"

"If you like."

Marjorie stepped toward the door. With a disgusted shrug Cindy stamped away. Marjorie turned the knob and pushed the reluctant door open.

She walked into a tiny study, the kind of place a

thoughtful parent might have rigged up for his daughters to use to do their homework. Felt-covered plywood laid across filing cabinets formed a makeshift desk against the back wall. Textbooks, spiral notebooks, and three-ring binders decorated with adolescent graffiti crammed a shelf above the desk. Posters of toothy young men with lots of hair whom Marjorie supposed she might have recognized if she'd ever watched the Fox network decorated the walls. In this room, the apparent epicenter of a charmed and golden early adolescence, Marjorie found Catherine.

Catherine was standing in the corner. She had her head bowed and her hands clasped behind her back at her waist, like a parody of Norman Rockwell that might have been titled *Schoolgirl in Disgrace*. A white kitchen timer ticked on the desk. The contrast between Catherine's penitent, juvenile posture and her matronly dress, sheer stockings, and elegant black flats seemed vaguely pornographic. Marjorie tried to banish an unwelcome mental image of lonely males in dreary hotel rooms flicking one-handed through magazines featuring pictures of scenes like this.

Catherine's shoulders stiffened and her ears pinkened when Marjorie entered the room, but Marjorie didn't see any other reaction to her presence. Catherine stood rigidly in place, stoically enduring her apparent penance.

"Catherine?" Marjorie said quietly. "Are you all right?"

No answer. No visible reaction.

"Is there anything I can do to help?"

No response.

"Satisfied?" Cindy asked icily from behind Marjorie. "Could you maybe just fuck off now and take a Metamucil break with your chums upstairs or something?"

"Is that your best idea under the circumstances?" Marjorie asked, turning to face Cindy.

"Look," Cindy said wearily. "Maybe you mean well and maybe I'm being a shit. But I've been through this before.

This is Cathy's trip. This goes on until she's ready for it to stop. The best thing you can do is leave. Tell your crew about our nice, dry basement and keep everyone else out of this room."

An abrupt rasp from the timer jerked their eyes back to the inside of the room. Turning from the corner, Catherine shut the timer off and without making eye contact with either Marjorie or Cindy walked wordlessly from the room. Cindy sighed and relaxed. Marjorie looked from Catherine's retreating figure back to Cindy.

"I don't have any right to ask this," Marjorie said, "but has this kind of thing been going on since your father died?"

"You're right. You don't have any right to ask that."

Her pace unconsciously quickening as she reached the stairs, Marjorie almost raced out of a clean, dry, semifinished basement that suddenly seemed creepily gothic.

She found Helmsing, Jenkins, and Wilcox huddled around the writing desk in the living room, poring over what looked like a building inspector's report.

"Oh, there you are," Helmsing said as she looked up. She immediately turned back to Jenkins. "I'll have a signed offer on your desk by Monday at noon. You'll find it very attractive."

"I'll look forward to it," Jenkins said.

" 'Attractive' is a relative term," Wilcox added casually. "I should warn you that you're not the only party who's recently expressed interest. I expect another offer to come in Monday morning. At or near the asking price, and without contingencies."

"Will I have a chance to beat it?" Helmsing asked.

"I'll do my best," Wilcox said, "but I can't guarantee it. The best thing would be for your first offer to be better than the other one I'm expecting."

"I'll keep that in mind," Helmsing said.

Seven

This has been an eventful Saturday," Marjorie said to Michaelson at what was in fact one o'clock the following Sunday morning. "But the last place I would have expected it to end up is Avery Phillips's condo."

"Knight to d-five," one of two males sharing the couch with them said to the other. Neither chessboard nor chessmen were in sight.

"I think the only reason Phillips finally returned my calls and halfway invited me over was that he assumed I'd bring you," Michaelson said.

He glanced again around the substantial gathering in the dim room, trying to spot Phillips. No luck. Knots of people here and there drank, smoked, and talked. Across the room a collection of guests seemed raptly engaged by the silent telecast of a basketball game. As background music they had chosen what you could call jazz if you weren't particular about music or English.

"Phillips apparently is going to make an offer Monday,"

Marjorie said, having already updated Michaelson on Friday's events at the Shepherd household. "That's what made Saturday eventful, and it should make Monday both busy and complicated."

"Busy I can appreciate, but why complicated?" Michaelson asked.

"Rook to e-seven," the other male on the couch said.

"Cindy wants to unload the place to any buyer who'll pay enough to keep her trust fund healthy. Catherine would prefer a residential buyer because she thinks that's what her dad would have wanted. The trustee doesn't care as long as no one can take her to court over it. And then there's Mrs. Shepherd."

"The girls' mother?"

"Yes. She's been living in California since she divorced their father. She has to be consulted too. The realtor told Patrice Helmsing, who told me during one of the eight dozen phone calls I fielded on this topic this afternoon."

"Told you because—" Michaelson prompted.

"Because she wants me to help her get the house," Marjorie explained. "Wilcox has set up a mass conference call for Monday afternoon. She's going to have everyone at the house on separate phones, Mom from California, and Phillips probably from here."

"It seems a bit baroque."

"She wants the entire discussion on the record," Marjorie said. "Literally. She's going to tape-record every word. If seller's remorse sets in after closing, she wants to be sure she doesn't get the blame."

"Fair enough. Then why can't Ms. Helmsing find a phone herself and get in on the call?"

"She'll be on the call, but from Detroit, where she has a speaking engagement. She wants me on the scene to make sure no one tries any funny business that couldn't be spotted over the phone."

"Which answers every question but one," Michaelson said. "Why has it suddenly become essential that a crucial conference call take place Monday afternoon instead of sometime when Ms. Helmsing could be physically present herself?"

"Because Ageless is playing hardball," Avery Phillips said as he strolled up. "I've already submitted an offer. If Wilcox doesn't accept it by five P.M. Monday, it's off the table. You'd have to have brass balls to walk away from it and she doesn't qualify—even metaphorically."

"Bishop to b-four," the male nearer Marjorie said.

"White to move and mate in two," Phillips said in his direction. "Now you kids quit showing off and run along. Go help Project with his basketball game. He took the Sonics and gave the points, and I understand the issue is in doubt."

"I gather, then," Marjorie said, "that I'm here to be told that Patrice Helmsing is wasting her time and mine in trying to get her hands instead of yours on Calvert Manor."

"Bingo. She can increase my cost but she can't get the house. I'm going to own it."

"It would be silly to ask you why you want it so badly," Michaelson mused. "If you wanted me to know the truth, you presumably wouldn't have lied in the first place. What I will ask is why the lie you picked was that nonsense about the European Union instead of something more straightforward that would have been harder for me to check?"

"Mischief," Phillips said. "Diplomatic allusion."

"Baloney," Michaelson said undiplomatically. "I think its appeal was precisely that I could check it and thereby provoke the kind of inquiries I did. You used me to get ostensibly independent information about your interest in Calvert Manor into the national security bureaucracy."

"Don't make things more complicated than they are,"

Phillips said. He made the comment with casual flippancy, but he couldn't keep his eyes from narrowing. "I thought the EU story was clever. Some junior analyst at Langley getting ambitious about your query on a slow day doesn't mean there are spooks in the shadows."

"How did Shepherd *père* die?" Michaelson asked abruptly.

"Suicide. Inoperable stomach cancer. Put his affairs carefully in order and blew his brains out. Thorough investigation by competent cops. No evidence of foul play. Next question."

"Do you suppose that when he was traveling regularly on business to Eastern Europe and the Soviet Union he made an occasional report stateside to one of those junior analysts you were just disparaging?"

"Oh, quit trying to make some two-bit hustling businessman into George Smiley," Phillips snapped bitchily. "It's tiresome and you're far too intelligent to believe it."

"Who said anything about George Smiley?" Michaelson asked amiably. "I know he wasn't picking up microfilm at newspaper kiosks or lingering in cafes waiting for agents in place. But like any number of public-spirited businesspeople and academics who traveled behind the Iron Curtain, he might very well have made trip reports: whether there was fresh fruit for sale on the street, whether the hotel clerks were cheerful or sullen—the kind of everyday stuff that junior analysts cut their teeth on."

"I can't help you with that. Langley and I haven't been on speaking terms since the mid-seventies."

"Well," Michaelson said, "if I were to start speculating on CIA interest in Calvert Manor, I'd start there."

"You're not thinking dispassionately," Phillips said. "You have an ego investment in an implausible theory and you don't like giving it up."

"I'm no longer being paid to think dispassionately," Michaelson said. "I can indulge personal likes and dislikes—and one thing I don't like is being used and lied to by someone from whom I have a right to expect better."

"It's a growth experience, Richard."

"So is a tumor. I'm not amused."

"Well, as we used to say in Vietnam," Phillips sighed with an elaborate shrug, " 'fuck 'em if they can't take a joke.' "

Michaelson and Marjorie stood up. Before either could come up with a snappy exit line, a vociferous commotion from the TV end of the room drew their attention. Blocking the television were Project, unmistakable even in the low light, and a stringy-haired man in his mid-twenties.

"I'm not paying till the fat lady sings," the man yelped. "There's *eighty-three seconds* left. Do you have any idea how many points an NBA team can score in eighty-three seconds?"

Project apparently did have quite detailed notions on this topic, for he immediately began to rattle off statistical data of impressive depth and pertinence. This proved to be more than his interlocutor could bear.

"Can the bullshit, you dumbass jock faggot," he began.

He did not continue. His choice of words was maladroit on several counts—count one being that he had to look up to spit them in Project's face. He didn't need to look up to see Project's left fist, which hit him in the solar plexus. The punch lifted him off the floor and propelled him about four feet across the room, where his now-descending body smashed an end table before landing on the floor amidst two years' copies of *Architectural Digest*.

"Praww-ject," Willie drawled in a nagging singsong, shaking his head and wagging his index finger in reprimand, "you've been a naughty homo."

Phillips, Michaelson, and Marjorie made their way over to the sprawled figure to confirm that he wasn't actually dead. As they came within convenient viewing distance, Marjorie still didn't recognize him, for she had never seen him before. She had no trouble, however, remembering when she had last seen the words silk-screened on the hot-pink T-shirt he was wearing: PRETTY GIRLS SMOKING CIGARETTES.

Eight

"You know," Marjorie said to Michaelson as they walked through sharp, clear, windless cold up Calvert Manor's driveway on Monday, "that's the first time I've ever seen anyone in Dockers work pants actually doing manual labor."

She was referring to Demarest, who was shoveling snow from the slightly pitched roof over Calvert Manor's verandah—if you can use a term as robust as "shoveling" to describe gingerly nudging clumps of snow toward the roof edge until gravity took over.

"Doing his bit, I suppose," Michaelson said.

Phillips's people were already there. Willie Gilchrist had dropped by on Phillips's behalf with Project in his wake—"just to make sure that nothing happens except on the telephone," as he was explaining to Wilcox, Catherine, Cindy, and C-Sharp when Marjorie and Michaelson stepped through the front door. This sounded a bit arch to Marjorie until she reflected that she had come to the house on Patrice Helmsing's behalf for basically the same reason.

"All right," Wilcox said briskly after rapid-fire amenities. "If everyone's here, we have less than ten minutes to get in place before the conference operator puts the call through."

Ten minutes struck Michaelson as more than ample for five people to find telephones in a house abundantly equipped with them, but this was reckoned without the nuanced choreography Wilcox apparently had in mind. She began passing around photocopied pages, which turned out to be annotated floor plans for Calvert Manor's first and second levels. Michaelson had seen seating charts for White House dinners that were less complicated.

"All right," Wilcox said. Again. "Ms. Randolph, I'd appreciate it if you'd use the telephone in the first-floor den. That's in the rear of the house. Mr. Gilchrist, you and, um, your friend are on the kitchen phone."

"Is this a black thing?" Willie trilled. After Wilcox gasped and a stricken expression washed across her face, Willie rolled his eyes theatrically over a wicked grin. "Joke, breeders. Hide the stuffed peppers, Project's in the kitchen with Willie."

"Okay," Wilcox said, breathing again. "All right. I'll be in the study at the rear of the second floor. Cindy, I have you down for your own bedroom, is that all right?"

"Sure," Cindy answered languidly. "I'm easy to please. Hi, Preston, nice pants."

Everyone glanced at Demarest, who, face flushed and a little damp, had just returned from his adventures on the porch roof. Catherine grabbed a cloth and sprang for the path he trod from the stairs, but Marjorie couldn't see any stains or water marks for her to wipe up. That didn't keep Catherine from dabbing a bit at the floor.

"All right," Wilcox insisted. "Where were we? Okay, Catherine. You wanted to be in the master bedroom, didn't you?"

"Yes," Catherine answered from her knees where she was rubbing a cloth over bone-dry parquet. "Preston has spread the repair and rehab records out in there, and I'd just as soon not move them."

"That's fine, sis," Cindy interjected in the same blase tone as before. "Just as long as Preston isn't in there with you—or in your own bedroom by himself."

"That's a bit Victorian, isn't it?" Catherine asked mildly.

"Bullshit," Cindy said cheerfully. "C-Sharp and company won't be with me, and there's no reason for Preston to be with you. He isn't in the will, he isn't in the bidding, and until he makes an honest woman of you, he isn't in the family. He doesn't have anything to say about what happens to this house, so he doesn't have any business being in on this conference call. I think Preston should be down here with C-Sharp."

"What a bore," Demarest said, shrugging. Then, looking at Wilcox, he asked, "What do you think?"

"*I* think you're being a spoiled brat," Willie said to Cindy. "You ought to be spanked."

"I really should," Cindy conceded with mock earnestness. "But Mom doesn't have the energy and C-Sharp doesn't have the imagination. And you don't look like you're up to it."

"On that particular topic I'm afraid I have nothing to contribute," Michaelson interjected after the ensuing silence approached an uncomfortable ten seconds. "My parents were liberals and I never had a posting to London."

"Honestly, Cindy," Catherine pleaded, "can't you skip the attitude for two hours?"

"Don't sweat it," Demarest said brusquely as he extended a protective arm toward Catherine. "It's not worth an uproar. Besides, I suppose that Cindy technically has a point. But how about if I use one of the guest bedrooms—

the front one, without a phone? Would that be okay with everyone?"

"Sure," Cindy said. "The wallpaper there goes with your socks, and there's plenty of light for you to read *Esquire* by."

"All right," Wilcox said, vastly relieved as she checked her watch again. "The people involved in the bidding are set. I don't care where the rest of you go, just stay off the phones."

"There's a buffet set up in the dining room," Catherine said, gesturing toward petit fours and sandwiches on crustless bread.

"Jesus Christ," Cindy said.

"All right," Wilcox said, her voice tinged with aggravation. "Remember, I'm recording the call and someone's writing me a big check when it's over, so let's get it right. Let's go."

They dispersed to their assigned places. An AT&T conference operator rang through on schedule and verified that everyone was ready: Avery Phillips at Fletcher Park; Patrice Helmsing in Detroit; Alison Shepherd in Palm Beach, California; and Willie, Marjorie, Wilcox, Cindy, and Cathy on extensions at Calvert Manor.

"All right," Wilcox said over the phone. "This will go more smoothly if you will please remember to identify yourselves when you speak, so that we all know who's talking and the tape's clear."

Marjorie heard a chorus of obedient assents. She glanced over at Michaelson, who had opened a slim volume of Peter Robinson's poetry and seemed settled in for a long siege.

"Very well," Wilcox said, dispensing for once with her standard exordium. "Tape is running. It's now 3:03 P.M., Eastern Standard Time. At this time we have a formal, written offer from Avery Phillips for two million six hundred thousand dollars for house, grounds, and *mobiliers antiques*. No financing condition, otherwise standard contingencies. Good through five P.M. local time today."

"What are we waiting for?" a female voice asked.

"Identify yourself please."

"Alison Shepherd. What are we waiting for? Let's take it."

"Catherine Shepherd," a voice said. "What are *mobiliers antiques*?"

"Movable furnishings more than one hundred years old, associated with the house but not physically attached."

"Catherine, still. We don't have anything like that, do we?"

"Alison Shepherd. Of course you don't. Let's go."

"This is Wilcox. As of ten o'clock this morning, we also have a formal, written offer from Patrice Helmsing. That offer is for two million six hundred twenty thousand dollars. House and grounds. Same contingencies."

"I'll match it."

"Identify—"

"Phillips," the intervening speaker snapped. "I'll match the money, and drop all contingencies. Two point six two at closing for a warranty deed and a bill of sale for the nonexistent antiques. Certified check or wire transfer."

"Hello? Everyone? This is Cindy."

"What is it, Cindy?" Wilcox asked.

"What's this contingency stuff? Can someone just run through that for me once?"

Marjorie threw her head back in silent exasperation while at least two voices contributed telephonic blasphemy to the proceedings. Wilcox began to explain title insurance, vested remainders, ground rent, mortgages, and adverse possession.

Michaelson glanced at Marjorie's rapidly glazing expression. He returned to Robinson, absorbing one more poem over the space of five minutes or so. Then he looked back at Marjorie, who hadn't spoken a syllable in the interval. Holding his hands a hopeful four inches apart, he raised his eyebrows questioningly. Marjorie shook her head and pinned the receiver to her shoulder with her cheek so that she could show Michaelson a full arm span.

Michaelson marked his place in the book, stood up, and left the room. He was a step and a half into the kitchen when Project spotted him and tapped Willie's shoulder.

"Whatsisname, Margie's boyfriend, on a stroll," Michaelson heard Willie say into the phone.

He didn't hear Phillips's response, but Marjorie reported it later: "If he heads upstairs, have Project stay with him."

Michaelson didn't go upstairs. He looked into the living room to verify that C-Sharp and friends were busy littering it with scraps from the dining-room collation. Then, shrugging for Willie's benefit, he started down the basement stairs.

He sought the basement not because he was bored to distraction, although he was, but because of Abraham Lincoln's classic argument about proving conspiracy by inference. You see a well-built house that four carpenters have worked on, Lincoln said—the door snug in its jamb, the nails countersunk in the boards, the windows tight in their frames—and you reasonably infer that it's not happenstance, that the four carpenters got together beforehand on what they were going to do.

The situation at Calvert Manor today seemed to Michaelson as cunningly contrived as any product of the joiner's art. Pieces put into place as neatly as dovetailed tongue and groove, fitted as precisely as mortise and tenon.

Wilcox and Cindy between them had managed to isolate the participants in the call from each other, and keep Demarest where he couldn't provide support or encouragement to Catherine. If Marjorie was right that Catherine would favor a residential sale, her isolation would help Phillips.

Michaelson reached the basement and began to wander through it. The colder air refreshed him. Things began to seem clearer.

Cindy and Wilcox might each help Phillips if they wanted to minimize the risk that Catherine's sentimentality would keep them from extracting the highest possible price for the property. Which was entirely possible. Demarest might tamely go along if he were a dimwit. Also possible. And no sense quibbling that only a few thousand dollars each could be at stake. Rich people debased themselves every day over petty amounts.

All of that, however, Michaelson reflected, still doesn't tell us why. What made Calvert Manor worth this kind of trouble to Phillips? Why did Phillips think he could sell this place at a profit when it had sat dormant on the market for months priced at less than he would now have to pay? Why, in other words, had Michaelson been used? What (if anything) did it have to do with Jim Halliburton's ruined mind and Michaelson's share of responsibility for it?

Michaelson didn't really expect to find the answer in the basement of Calvert Manor. When he did find it, though, he suspected it would have more to do with the Shepherd family than with the home they lived in. He was down here to get a sense of that family, to feel himself the eerie tension Marjorie had mentioned when she described Cathy's reversion to preadolescence.

Marjorie's directions had been clear, and he quickly came to the room where Catherine had stood in the corner. It struck him immediately as more than a forgotten childhood venue. As his gaze ranged over the juvenilia that filled the room, in fact, he decided that "forgotten" was exactly the wrong word. On the contrary, it seemed more like a museum exhibit, each detail gotten painstakingly right. The memorial of a dead childhood, frozen morbidly in time like the bedroom of a dead child.

Perhaps it was because of this reflection that the row of spiral notebooks next to the three-ring binders on the shelf above the desk seemed out of place the second time he looked at them. At least the ones nearer the end did. They looked newer and less timeworn than they should have. He had come down here to feel rather than to search, but the anomaly piqued his curiosity. He pulled down the last notebook.

He could still read "Revco $2.89" on a price tag stuck to its back. Would Catherine have continued to study in this room even when she was a junior or senior in high school? Unlikely. Assume she had, though, and $2.89 still struck Michaelson as a bit pricey for eight or nine years in the past.

He flicked the notebook's pages until he came to the last one with writing. Neatly handwritten in its top margin was last Thursday's date—the day of the corner episode. Filling the lines below was a sentence written and rewritten repeatedly:

> I MUST NOT BREAK MY WORD AFTER I HAVE GIVEN IT.
> I MUST NOT BREAK MY WORD AFTER I HAVE GIVEN IT.
> I MUST NOT BREAK MY WORD AFTER I HAVE GIVEN IT.

The reproachful self-admonition appeared twenty times on that page and an equal number on the four preceding pages, each with the same date.

He flipped to the front of the notebook. The first page was dated in September of the previous year—a little over six months ago. The repeated sentence on that page was shorter:

I MUST NOT BE SELF-CENTERED.

"Just a misdemeanor, apparently," Michaelson reflected aloud as he counted only twenty-five iterations.

With growing fascination, Michaelson went page by page through the notebook.

October 2nd: I MUST NOT BE PETULANT. Written fifty times.

October 19th: I MUST OFFER ONLY CONSTRUCTIVE CRITICISM. Written one hundred times.

November 1st: I MUST NOT LOSE MY TEMPER OVER MINOR MATTERS. One hundred times.

November 11th: I MUST NOT BE UNDULY CRITICAL OF OTHERS' EFFORTS. One hundred times.

November 16th: I MUST NOT FORGET APPOINTMENTS. Fifty times.

December 4th: I MUST NOT WASTE TIME IN FRIVOLOUS PURSUITS. Twenty-five times.

And on and on. At least twice a month, sometimes twice a week. In the oddly captivating procession of self-inflicted chastisements, one in particular caught Michaelson's attention. Dated February 3, a little over five weeks before, it read:

I MUST BE MORE CONSIDERATE OF THE FEELINGS OF PEOPLE WHO CARE ABOUT ME.

Stretching with grinding monotony over the fronts and backs of ten solid pages, the sentence was written five hundred times.

Feeling somewhat guilty and not a little mean, Michaelson tore a blank page from the back of the notebook. He noted each date that appeared in the book and wrote out the sentence written under that date and the number of times it was repeated. When he had finished, he replaced the notebook on its shelf and folded the results of his own copy work into his suit coat, wondering if he'd get the remorseful urge tonight to sit at his desk and write I MUST RESPECT THE PRIVACY OF OTHERS one hundred times.

Probably not, he concluded.

His little finger felt damp and gritty where he had rested it on the desk while he copied Catherine's penances. He looked at the desk, where water smears darkened a few square inches of the black burlap surface, with white granules scattered over them.

Cocaine? He captured several granules with the tip of his index finger and tasted them. Table salt. No surprise. After all, he hadn't found any evidence of Catherine writing I MUST NOT CONSUME HARMFUL AND ILLEGAL SUBSTANCES.

Glancing at his watch, Michaelson was astonished to see that over forty-five minutes had passed since he'd left Marjorie. He'd stolen a long peek at what looked like the diary of a very elaborate neurosis, and he felt he knew a lot more about the Shepherds than he had when he'd come downstairs. But he still didn't have much of a handle on what Avery Phillips's game was.

Oh well, he thought, as he started up the stairs. Maybe after all this time they've sold the house to Patrice Helmsing.

That's when he heard, faintly filtered through two floors but nevertheless unmistakable, the shrill, piercing ululations of a smoke detector's alarm.

Nine

Mental images of flame-engulfed rooms and hallways choked with thick smoke quickened Michaelson's steps as he hustled up from the basement. An elemental reflex, an instinctive fear going back to Homo sapiens' most distant ancestors, screamed "GET OUT!" As he stepped into the kitchen he struggled to master the panicky urge.

An uproar from the living room suggested chaos amidst a general rush for the door. In the kitchen itself, by contrast, Willie showed no signs of panic. Joined to the alarm's piercing wail were hysterical screams coming from the second floor.

"I've told the conference operator to call nine-one-one and have anyone in the time zone with a siren get over here," Willie was telling Marjorie, who looked like she had rushed in a few moments before Michaelson. "Project, quit looking for the fire extinguisher. If you haven't found it by now, you're not going to turn it up."

"That scream's coming from upstairs," Marjorie said.

"Right," Willie said. "Let's go, Project."

He began racing up the main staircase with Project behind him, followed by Michaelson and Marjorie. They skirted past Wilcox, who was scrambling down, cradling a hastily stuffed briefcase in one arm and a tape recorder in the other.

The first thing they saw on the second floor was Cindy trying to wrestle Catherine away from the guest bedroom door. Still screaming, Catherine writhed in her sister's grasp. Wisps of smoke seeped insidiously from the cracks between the top and upper sides of the door and the jamb, gathering in a thin haze near the hallway ceiling. It was the hallway smoke detector that was screeching.

"Get her out of here," Willie ordered as Marjorie stepped toward the two young women and Michaelson tried the door.

"Locked," he announced. The hallway smoke stung his tearing eyes. "Not hot to the touch."

Marjorie clapped her left hand gently but firmly over Catherine's mouth and squeezed her nose shut with her right thumb and forefinger while Cindy continued to pin her struggling sister's arms. Catherine's eyes widened almost cartoonishly. The screams stopped as she ran out of wind.

"Hush," Marjorie murmured, trying to make her near-whisper as soothing as she could. "Let's go downstairs."

After what her livid face suggested was a moment's terrified incomprehension, Catherine nodded. Awkwardly but without resistance Cindy and Marjorie began to walk her toward the stairs.

Michaelson went into the bathroom that adjoined the guest bedroom. He tried the connecting door after a long touch told him the bottom panel was room temperature. The knob turned freely, but something stubbornly blocked the door as he tried to push it open.

He scurried back into the hall. Smoke was now gathering faster. Project rubbed his shoulder as he and Willie anxiously inspected a solid-looking hallway door.

"The lock doesn't seem as tight in here," Michaelson barked.

Four seconds later, Project was in a crouch, his right foot braced against the side of the bathtub. He launched himself toward the connecting door. His massive right shoulder slammed into it just beside the knob. That side of the door yielded perceptibly, and a noise compounded of shearing metal and cracking wood came from the other side.

Eyes streaming, Project stepped back, calmly resumed his stance, and charged again. The unmistakable crack of splintering wood reached them, and the door cleared the jamb by an inch or two.

Smoke began to flow in earnest into the bathroom. Michaelson jumped to open the bathroom window. When he looked back, Willie and Project had pushed the door all the way open and Willie was bulling into the bedroom with Project following.

Smoke seemed to fill the bedroom. A choking, dark gray fog billowed near the ceiling, thinning to a gauzy film below chest level.

Michaelson at first saw no fire at all. It took him another moment or two to spot the source of the smoke. Squinting, he could see smoke pumping from the fireplace next to the window. Two or three tongues of flame licked at the back of the charred logs and kindling still stacked in the fireplace itself.

The window next to the fireplace was closed. Handkerchief pressed over his mouth, crouching below the worst of the smoke, Michaelson crossed quickly to the window and strained against the lower frame in an effort to open it. The thermal pane moved up perhaps three inches and stopped. Every ounce of muscle Michaelson had, straining from the soles of his feet, couldn't budge it another millimeter.

Demarest's body lay near the fireplace, his head resting on the stonework just in front of it. His pants and underpants were bunched around his ankles. The hem of his shirt only partially hid his penis and testicles. Willie grabbed Demarest's legs and Project his shoulders. They lugged him awkwardly toward the bathroom door.

Michaelson felt the acrid smoke beginning to sear his throat as the draft from the window sucked the stuff down from the ceiling and outside. As a ragged cough racked his lungs, he waved through the smoke, hurried around Willie and Project, and swung the connecting door completely open for them. In ten fretful seconds, Willie and Project managed to get Demarest through the bathroom and into the hallway.

The hallway held much less smoke than the bedroom, and that was apparently all Project needed. With a grunt he siung Demarest's body across his shoulders and began lumbering down the stairs.

Michaelson remembered nothing but Project's muscular legs and rear end until, standing shin-deep in the snow that still covered Calvert Manor's front lawn, he put his hands on his knees and convulsively gulped blessedly sharp winter air into his lungs. He must have seen Marjorie attempting mouth-to-mouth resuscitation with Demarest because he recalled it later, but the image didn't register with him consciously until afterward. For the moment he concentrated on wondering when the interesting black and red spots were going to stop dancing in front of his eyes.

The keening peal of sirens drew closer. Less than a minute passed before a fire truck and an EMT van hurtled into the driveway and then onto the front lawn. His eye drawn by the approaching siren, Michaelson glanced up long enough to see Willie fishing a black leather key case unobtrusively from Demarest's trousers. Moments later Demarest lay on a gurney with a plastic mask pressed over his face and Michaelson was again bent over and taking deep breaths.

Two goggled, oxygen-masked firemen scrambled up a ladder toward the pair of windows with smoke pouring from them. The first to reach the verandah roof crab-walked to the guest bedroom window, smashed the lower pane with the base of a fire extinguisher, and gunned a long blast of white foam into the room from the fire extinguisher's cone. Then he disappeared into the billows of now-charcoal smoke that seemed to explode through the opening. His colleague quickly followed.

"What were you doing up there, explaining the Treaty of Westphalia to everybody?" Marjorie asked.

"Everything just seemed to take a long time," Michaelson panted apologetically. "Willie and Project did a lot more than I did."

"Well, Willie's chatting on a cellular phone and Project's looking on with avid attention, so offhand I'd say they're in better shape than you are."

"Hold that thought," Michaelson said in a nearly normal voice.

He straightened and looked around. Wilcox stood on the driveway with C-Sharp and his entourage. Two med-techs were loading Demarest and the gurney into the back of the van. Catherine, standing about eight feet away, strained toward the van as she saw Demarest slipped into it. Cindy subtly held her back.

"Running hot," Michaelson commented as red lights began to flash on the back.

"Just for the exercise," Marjorie said quietly.

"You don't think he's going to make it?"

"I think he already hasn't made it. I'm no Kay Scarpetta,

but I'd bet my store's stock of Patricia Cornwell hardcovers that I was blowing air into a corpse just now."

A police car pulled into the driveway.

"May I borrow your cell phone?" Michaelson asked Marjorie.

"You're thinking of something foolish, aren't you?" Marjorie demanded, slipping the tiny phone into his jacket pocket.

"Thank you. Are you up to a ladylike scream?"

"That's an oxymoron," Marjorie said. She nevertheless produced a quite creditable yelp as Michaelson offered a gingerly semblance of collapsing and stretched out in the snow.

The police officer noticed him immediately and rapped urgently on the back of the EMT van. Seventy seconds later Michaelson, blanketed on a gurney, was being loaded into the van next to Demarest. The van peeled away with its siren screaming as soon as the door slammed.

The officer walked over to the fireman still waiting at the base of the ladder and talked with him. After what seemed like an hour and a half and was probably closer to eight minutes, the two firemen who'd gone through the guest bedroom came out of the front door of Calvert Manor. Their oxygen masks now dangled from their necks and their goggles were parked over the visors of their helmets. They joined the pair of men at the base of the ladder. Following ninety seconds or so of confabulation, the police officer and the fireman who'd been waiting outside walked over to Marjorie.

"Are you the owner?" he asked.

"No," Cindy said, striding up. "I am. And my sister and mother. It's kind of complicated."

The fireman's expression suggested scant interest in the intricacies of joint tenancy.

"It looks like someone started a fire in the bedroom fireplace with the damper closed. We've saturated the logs, opened the damper, opened some more upstairs windows to let the smoke out, and turned the furnace off."

"Okay," Cindy said.

"My men tell me there's a smoke alarm in the bedroom that apparently didn't go off. How often do you check the batteries?"

"Don't have a clue." Cindy shrugged.

"Do you change the batteries in all the smoke detectors at the same time?"

"I don't really take care of it," Cindy said. "How long before we can go back in the house?"

"You can go back inside now to get out of the cold," the fireman said. "But stay on the first floor, in the living room. We have to make a report, and a fire marshal's going to come out and take some statements."

"Why?" Cindy asked.

Because I've won my bet, Marjorie thought.

"My sister needs to be looked at by a doctor right away," Cindy said in a low, urgent plea, pushing closer to the cop as she spoke. "That was her fiancé on the meat wagon, and that Valium the techie fed her isn't going to last fifteen minutes."

"If you want to call your family doctor, it's fine with me," the officer said. "And if it looks like she needs it, I can get another ambulance out here. But right now I need to ask all of you to please move on inside and wait in the living room."

The separate groups began shuffling toward the porch. As they bunched together near the front door, Marjorie saw Willie edge close to Wilcox. Without making a production of it, Marjorie strained to catch their exchange:

"Ageless says to tell you assign the insurance proceeds

and the offer's still good till midnight tonight," Willie said.

"Auction rules," Wilcox said, shaking her head. "The hammer never fell. We have to start over from square one."

Ten

Would you take this, please?" Michaelson said to the med-tech, tendering a plastic oxygen mask. "I'm not sure where it goes."

"It goes over your nose and mouth till we get to the ER," the man said. "And lie back down. I'm in for beaucoup paperwork if you kick off before I wheel you out."

"No danger of that. I'm perfectly all right, really."

He pulled Marjorie's cell phone from beneath the blanket covering him and punched in one of the numbers he carried in his head.

"It's four miles of undiluted oxygen makes you think you're all right," the med-tech said. "But they'll want to hold you overnight for observation."

"I'm a competent adult with minimum insurance and I decline to be observed."

Before the med-tech could offer any rebuttal a breathless female voice informed Michaelson that he had reached Cavalier Books.

"Ah, Carrie, there you are," he said into the phone.

"Two things. First, Ms. Randolph will be delayed. Second, would you do me the immense favor of calling a taxi to meet me at MRTC? . . . Nothing has happened to her except that she's gotten a bit chilly, but she's probably going to have to spend several more hours out at Calvert Manor answering rather tiresome questions. . . . There's a girl, thank you, Carrie."

He looked back toward the med-tech as he replaced the phone.

"I notice you haven't devoted much attention to my quiet friend here," he said.

"Can't help him," the med-tech said. "Never made it to the seminary. And I can't help you much, 'cause they don't let med-techs practice psychiatry in Maryland."

Siren wailing and lights flashing, the ambulance still needed another twelve minutes to negotiate the snow-snarled way to the Maryland Regional Trauma Center. As it backed up to the receiving dock, the med-tech glanced out a side window.

"Your cab is just pulling in," he said, shaking his head. "You know, I do believe that was about the most high-handed performance I've ever seen."

"You've led a sheltered life," Michaelson said with a brief smile as he exited the ambulance. "You ought to see an ambassador's wife in action sometime."

The twenty bone-jolting minutes that it took the taxi to reach Demarest's address were just enough for the cabbie's explanation, in precise but heavily accented English, of the fatal shortsightedness infecting America's attitude toward NATO expansion. A growing sense of urgency doing more damage to his arteries than smoke inhalation ever could have, Michaelson barely refrained from pointing out that Riga wasn't crawling with cabbies who discussed foreign policy in American-accented Latvian.

Cloaking his *hurry-up-dammit* impulses behind a mask of

measured serenity, he deliberately slowed his pace as he approached the door of the flat above Demarest's. Its no-nonsense denizen had had ample time to spot him as he walked from curbside to porch, and to recall his suspicious visit of a few days before. He was pleasantly surprised when she answered his buzz not with a warning shot but by asking him over the speaker what he wanted.

"I'm afraid I have some unpleasant news," he said. "May I come in?"

"No. Spill it."

"There's been a fire at Calvert Manor. Mr. Demarest has been taken to Maryland Regional Trauma Center."

Almost instantly he heard hurrying steps clomping down the stairway inside the door. The expression on the face that thrust itself at him when the door flew open was simultaneously stricken and accusing.

"How bad?" she demanded.

"I can't be certain," he said. "Smoke inhalation."

She looked at Michaelson with intense concentration for a moment, as if trying to decipher from his eyes truth that she wasn't hearing in his words.

"You're his mother, aren't you?" Michaelson said gently. "I'm very sorry."

"How did you know?"

"Not many tenants guard their landlords' property with Horatian intensity," Michaelson said. "And once I got the idea that you were more than a tenant, the family resemblance seemed plain. Then I indirectly confirmed it through him."

"I have to go there," she said brusquely, pushing past him and closing the door tightly behind her.

"By all means. Before you do, though, there's something you should know."

"What's that?" she asked, turning back toward Michaelson.

"Some men are going to come to search his apartment. Soon. If there's anything in there that you don't want these men to find, now would be an excellent time to remove it."

"Police?"

"Eventually," Michaelson said, "but the men I'm talking about definitely aren't police, and they'll be here a lot sooner."

"How do you know they'll be coming?" she asked.

"Because I saw one of them take Mr. Demarest's keys out of his pocket before he was put in the ambulance."

Agonizing indecision etched eloquently across her features, the woman gazed in baleful suspicion at Michaelson. If only she could figure out some way to blame all this on him, her expression seemed to say, everything would be much clearer. Finally her eyes snapped twice and her face took on a decisive cast. She scampered across the porch to Demarest's door.

Michaelson moved to the far end of the porch and waited. He crossed his arms, then unabashedly promoted the arm cross to a full-scale hug while he stamped his feet. Stoicism was fine to a point, but he was getting cold. In a perverse way, he supposed, this was apropos; for the thought of what he was about to do chilled his belly as much as the boreal wind did his fingers and toes.

The woman was inside Demarest's apartment for seven minutes—long enough to get selected things she knew were there, but not to search the place. Michaelson moved toward the sound of the opening door and gallantly held it open for her as she came out, awkwardly laden with a grocery sack pressed against her chest. He braced his free hand against the inside door.

"I don't want the money or the drugs," Michaelson said quietly when he saw that he had her attention. "But I have to have the envelopes."

80

"What envelopes?" she demanded.

"Please," he sighed. "Your son took deliveries at a New York Avenue club from people who arrived on foot without handcarts. Hence drugs, therefore money. But the men coming here don't care about that either. They're interested in something else. So am I. Now, it's getting late. I'm cold and you're in a hurry. Let's get it done."

This decision she made quickly. Carefully concealing the remaining contents of the sack from Michaelson, she extracted a pale yellow civil service routing envelope.

"There was only one," she said as he took it from her.

Michaelson thanked her, but she had already turned away and moved off.

Michaelson stepped into Demarest's apartment, closed the door firmly, and made himself comfortable in a leather armchair near a heating register before he opened the envelope. The first thing he found was a strip of tiny negatives looped repeatedly around a long, narrow rectangle of white cardboard.

Lord, he mused, I thought Minoxes went out with Nehru jackets. He unlooped the strip and held it up to the pale white sunlight infiltrating the room through the window behind his chair. He couldn't begin to make out any detail, but he saw enough to satisfy him that the first sixteen shots were of one document laid at a slight angle on top of another—just like the documents in the photograph Halliburton had sent him.

The other thing in the envelope was a carbon copy of a three-page document headed DESK MEMO. From Lancer to File, according to the heading, Re: Assorted Debriefings. Dated July 1, 1987. Andrew Shepherd showed up at the top of page two. The memo called him Professor, but the details reported left no doubt about his identity: "In-country 12–20 June. No significant contact GOY. Main visit = Jessenice. Incredibly crowded (locals—'some religious crap'), every decent hotel booked, had to share room at Peace & Friendship Hostel ('total fleabag'). Aus/Czech goods readily available street markets."

Michaelson had no trouble sorting through the telegraphic data. "GOY" was Government of Yugoslavia, whose representatives had avoided Andrew Shepherd on this particular trip. Shepherd had come to Jessenice and stayed at a world-class hotel with all the amenities and a price tag to match. Then he had come back to the United States and told Lancer that an influx of Yugoslav religious enthusiasts had forced him to put up with squalid student accommodations.

"Lancer" was one of the trade names used at the Central Intelligence Agency by Aldrich Ames. Michaelson happened to know that, but even if he hadn't, he could have figured it out. Josh Logan had gotten Halliburton's document to Michaelson the evening of February 23, 1994, and the next morning *The New York Times* had reported the FBI's arrest of Aldrich Ames for espionage. That had begun the public exposure of Ames as the CIA's now-notorious Soviet mole, who soon afterward cut a deal to save his neck and began serving life in prison for selling his country's secrets.

Michaelson roused himself sternly from his reverie, for company was coming and there was work to do before it arrived. Even with a flurry of activity, however, he couldn't entirely avoid a moment's introspection.

"What a pathetic thing to die for," he muttered as he searched for a fresh envelope.

Eleven

"Y" ou're sure about the color?" the detective asked Marjorie twenty minutes into his interview with her.

"Yes," Marjorie said. "The smoke definitely changed color when the blast from the fire extinguisher hit it."

The detective was certainly the most junior of the three plainclothes officers who had shown up at Calvert Manor a little over half an hour after the ambulance had sped off. He flicked longish and unruly straw-colored hair with a quick head shake as he tapped at a notebook computer on his lap. Marjorie had no trouble imagining what Inspector Morse would have thought about the laptop. Or about people scattered in knots around the first floor, chatting desultorily while they waited for the cops to get around to them.

Another detective, who could shake his head all day long without flicking any hair, sauntered over and glanced down at his younger colleague's screen.

"Whaddaya got?" he asked.

"In the den. Didn't see anyone go upstairs. Didn't notice anyone get off the call. Smoke changed color."

"What about this?" He handed the seated man a Baggie.

"Do you know of any reason why this would have been lying outside in the snow?" the guy with the laptop asked.

"No," Marjorie said.

"Did you notice anyone running away from the *back* of the house after the smoke alarm went off?"

"No," Marjorie said, "but I had other things on my mind."

"I understand. Did you notice anyone with the original group inside who didn't turn up outside?"

"No. I mean everyone that I knew inside turned up outside, but I'm afraid I didn't pay that much attention to the musicians." Marjorie examined the Baggie. She didn't know what drug residue looked like, but if there was anything at all on the soggy plastic bag, she couldn't see it.

"Another witness said that you were here a few days ago with someone who was looking at the house," the older detective said.

"That's true," Marjorie said. "Patrice Helmsing. And before that with Richard Michaelson. And once on my own before today."

"That's a very precise recollection," the younger detective said. Smiling. Encouraging. Challenging.

"I can't hide my own Easter eggs yet," Marjorie said.

"Okay," the younger cop said. The right collar tip on his aqua Izod curled upward and he tried unsuccessfully to flatten it. "I'll try to have a preliminary statement written up for you in twenty minutes or so. We'd appreciate it if you could wait to review it and sign it before you leave."

Marjorie left the two detectives at the far end of the living room and strode toward the dining room, less in search of lobster paste on crustless bread than to stretch her legs. And to think.

She didn't know why it was important that the smoke had changed color, but that should be easy enough to find out. *Criminalistics and Scientific Crime Investigation* by Cunliffe and Piazza was buried somewhere in deep stock at Cavalier Books, and if that didn't have the answer, Carrie could find a tome somewhere in Georgetown University's libraries that would.

From the look of it, the Baggie had been found outside in the snow, which might be interesting or might just mean that a band member had dumped evidence of contraband pharmaceuticals once it was clear the cops were coming.

What was most interesting, though, was that three detectives and a scene-of-crime team had hustled out to Calvert Manor less than an hour after a patrolman learned that Preston Demarest had died in a room with a smoky fireplace. Marjorie wasn't sure how this type of thing played out in country houses in Sussex or elsewhere in the land of English detectives. In suburban Maryland, however, the implication was clear: This wasn't an arson investigation; it was a murder investigation.

She ate a minislice of smoked ham on an egg roll for form's sake. Then she ate another one because she was hungry after the first. She was actually eyeing tiny triangles of spinach quiche when she realized that she was unconsciously avoiding a painful visit to Catherine in the den. The upstairs had still been off-limits when everyone went back into the house, and Cindy had led Catherine into the den to rest while the sedatives worked.

Collecting three sandwiches on a napkin, Marjorie quietly entered the darkened room. Catherine lay on the couch where Marjorie had sat during the conference call. Her shoes were on the floor. A pale blue comforter covered her from foot to chin. Beneath a damp, folded facecloth on her forehead, her wide open eyes stared vacantly at the ceiling. On the telephone table at the head of the couch, a dove-gray teacup on a matching saucer sat next to a teapot under an embroidered cozy.

Catherine didn't react at all to Marjorie's entrance. Marjorie went over to the couch and crouched beside the younger woman.

"You look like you're being very well taken care of."

"Cindy," Catherine said, as if the two syllables required enormous effort.

"Would you like to eat anything?"

Catherine answered with a minute shake of her head.

"It's a shame to let this tea go to waste," Marjorie said. Putting the sandwiches down, she picked up the saucer. "It's still nice and hot. Cindy must have freshened it up just a couple of minutes ago. Why don't you try some?"

Marjorie moved the cup close enough to Catherine for the fragrance of orange pekoe to waft toward her nose. The barest flicker of animation flashed in her eyes. She propped herself laboriously up on one elbow and sipped as Marjorie lifted the cup to her lips. The sip turned into several enthusiastic swallows before Catherine lay back contentedly.

"That was heaven," she whispered in something much closer to a normal voice. "Thank you."

"You're welcome. Are you sure you wouldn't like a sandwich?"

"No, thank you," Catherine said. "I'm afraid I'm about to drift off to sleep again."

"That sounds like an excellent idea."

Marjorie put the cup and saucer back on the telephone table, replaced the compress on Catherine's forehead, and tucked the comforter back around her shoulders. By the time Marjorie had gotten to her feet, Catherine's eyes were closed and her breathing had turned rhythmic and peaceful.

She knows, Marjorie thought. She knows Demarest is dead.

Catherine might have figured this out in the front yard, the same way Marjorie had. But Catherine hadn't looked like she was in any condition for even that modest level of cogitation at the time.

The other possibility was that Cindy had found a way to break the news to her. And if so, it seemed to Marjorie that that was one of the sanest and kindest things Cindy could have done—exactly the way Marjorie would want to be treated when (not if, she acknowledged to herself, given their age difference) the time came for her to get bad news about Michaelson.

On reflection, in fact, it struck Marjorie that the only significant word in her conversation with Catherine had been ''Cindy.'' Not just Cindy taking care of Catherine in her immediate distress, but Cindy doing all those un-Cindy-like things that would mean something to Catherine: thinking to take her sister's shoes off, digging the comforter out of some forgotten drawer or closet, making the compress, brewing the tea, using a cozy to keep the pot warm, serving the tea in an elegant cup and saucer instead of a utilitarian mug, freshening the tea in the cup as it cooled. Things that were striking not because they were large but precisely because they were small. Small things done well. The kinds of things you wouldn't think your way to in the stress of a crisis. Things that had to emerge from habits of mind and heart deliberately bred and carefully ripened over years of lives shared. Marjorie was still mulling over this unfamiliar image of Cindy as she withdrew from the den and headed for the nearest downstairs bathroom. She didn't have the slightest notion of eavesdropping. It was just that when she found the door closed she thought it best to find out if someone else was inside. She raised her hand for a discreet knock when she heard C-Sharp's voice.

"All right, all right. She's strung out to hell and back. I just thought a little happy dust later on might help, that's all."

"Don't think, it's not your strong suit." Cindy's voice.

"You don't have to get pissy about it."

"Don't whine until I'm through chewing your ass out," Cindy said. "Just listen. Get this straight. You do not *ever* offer drugs to Catherine. Not crack, not 'ludes, not Ecstasy, not pot, not Jack Daniels, not Miller Lite. You do not make jokes about it. You do not talk about it. You do not think about it."

"Okay, okay, I—"

"Shut up. You do not even *begin* to think about it. *If* you find yourself thinking about it, you get a hammer and hit yourself in the balls until you *stop* thinking about it. You got that?"

"Yes—OOF! *Jesus*, Cindy!"

"Good. Because if you don't, I will."

There might have been more, but Marjorie figured she had the gist. She decided to go in search of other facilities.

Twelve

"Colonel Mustard in the bedroom with the fireplace. What a precious little cliché this is turning into."

Michaelson had the satisfaction of seeing Avery Phillips give the front room of Demarest's flat a deer-in-the-headlights look as Michaelson offered this comment from the corner armchair. Phillips had just come in and the disposable surgical gloves on his hands suggested that he had been expecting solitude.

"Aren't you glad to see me, A.P.?" Michaelson asked. "You look as jumpy as a gambler holding aces and eights with his back to the door. And where are Willie and Project, by the way?"

"Keeping their eyes open nearby in case the police get ambitious enough to take a look at this place before tomorrow morning. There's another jurisdiction involved, so I don't really expect that kind of company tonight, but you can't be too careful."

"Quite right," Michaelson said with a diffident smile.

"And as long as we're asking by-the-way questions: What are you doing here, by the way?"

"Searching for the same thing you are. The difference is that I found it."

"Where is it?" Phillips asked.

"In the custody of the United States Postal Service, addressed to me at the Brookings Institution. And don't think about intercepting it, because you can't. Not that it would be worth the trouble."

"You'll have to do better than that," Phillips said with a knife-flick smile as he started opening drawers in a small desk near the door.

"Search the place if you want to," Michaelson said, rising. "I've waited a good forty minutes for you because I thought we should talk as soon as possible. But if you'd rather waste your time verifying what I've just told you, we can talk tomorrow."

"Talk about what?" Phillips asked as he stopped rifling the drawer.

"Two things. First: the substance of the document you would have found if I hadn't beaten you to it—which I will tell you. Second and more important: what you're actually up to in this little adventure—which you will tell me."

"Deal," Phillips said. "You first."

Michaelson summarized the Lancer memo in four clipped sentences.

"What a bombshell," Phillips exclaimed a bit theatrically when Michaelson had finished. "You can't imagine how cross I am about getting here too late to cop a prize like that."

"Oh please," Michaelson said. He smiled in spite of himself.

"Don't scoff," Phillips said, raising an admonitory index finger. "There's something you don't know, although with the hints from that memo you'd find it out soon enough. Sometime in the mid-eighties a very holy woman died in a mountain village not far from Jessenice. Near the Austrian border. Catholic area. Imbued with piety and all that. The customary reports of miracles and visions and so forth followed. The village became a pilgrimage site."

"Hence the memo's reference to 'religious crap,' " Michaelson said. "If Jessenice were jammed to the gills during the off-season, which for an alpine area would be late spring and summer, that would imply huge numbers of pilgrims and therefore an upsurge in religious interest and practice."

"And a head-grabbing increase in papal influence. All of which would be very bad news for commies, who you may remember tried to bump His Holiness off not many years before all this happened. Balkan Reds being the cringing little shits they are, a lot of them might have been inclined to cut their losses after getting information like this."

"Very elegant," Michaelson said.

"Well, you do see it, don't you?" Phillips demanded impatiently. "Andrew Shepherd, who I'll bet never stayed anywhere that didn't have every amenity from CNN International in English on down, told Lancer a fairy tale about some youth hostel. This false information had enormous potential political significance. He did that because someone told him to. Fill in the blanks."

"Lancer was Aldrich Ames. Your turn."

"Stop being difficult. You know this as well as I do."

"Humor me," Michaelson said.

"Someone at the CIA," Phillips said with elaborate patience after pursing his lips in exasperation for a moment, "used this innocuous American businessman to give phony data to Aldrich Ames, and therefore to his Soviet paymasters, several years before Ames was formally exposed as a commie spy. Ergo, Langley knew for years that Ames was spying for the Reds and let him keep on spying so that we could peddle grade A bullshit to the Kremlin."

"But all this time Ames was of course also giving the Russians some genuine information," Michaelson said.

"Right. Which meant real human beings spying for the United States in the Soviet Union got a bullet in the back of the neck at Lubayanka Prison. But you can't make omelets without breaking eggs, can you? I can just hear one of the old bastards saying it: 'I hated losing them, but I would have hated losing Germany more.' "

"And your own involvement?" Michaelson prompted.

"Isn't it obvious? This is page one stuff. Above the fold."

"So?" Michaelson asked. "Are you looking for a job with the *Post?*"

"Of course not. I'm a real-estate broker. Calvert Manor is a piece of real estate. Buried somewhere in its bowels is documentation of this story, which the Central Intelligence Agency hopes never comes to light. So I buy the place."

"After meanwhile using me to let the CIA know that you're surreptitiously after that property."

"Well, yes, technically," Phillips said. "I suppose 'used' isn't an entirely inappropriate term. Excuse me for not being embarrassed about that."

"In any event . . ." Michaelson prompted.

"In any event, not wanting me to stumble over the documentation, the CIA takes the shack off my hands for, say, a hundred fifty percent of what I pay for it. After modest expenses I pocket a profit of over a million dollars."

Michaelson turned toward Phillips with an appreciative smile.

"Congratulations," he said. "That was quite well done, especially for an extemporaneous presentation. I particularly liked that little moue with your lips near the beginning."

"Are you suggesting that what I just said wasn't entirely truthful?" Phillips demanded in icily precise enunciations.

"No," Michaelson said. "I'm suggesting that it's utter rot."

"What an odd comment," Phillips said, his face a picture of bafflement. "You're not normally quite that silly."

"I'm referring to your premise, of course. That first bit about using Aldrich Ames as a disinformation agent is quite plausible. But any notion that the CIA would pay you off to keep the story under wraps is nonsense."

"I keep hoping for an interval of lucidity in this conversation, and you keep disappointing me. Trust me: Spooks don't want their treachery publicized."

"Sensible spooks would rather be thought treacherous than inept," Michaelson said. "Aldrich Ames is the most devastating professional and public relations disaster the CIA has ever experienced. You think you can prove that leaving Ames on the job wasn't blithering incompetence but cold-blooded realpolitik. The CIA wouldn't pay a penny to spike that story. If you actually managed to get the theory in play, in fact, they'd drop enough hints to Safire to give the thing some legs. There's something connected with Calvert Manor that you hope to sell to someone who gets information through the national security apparatus. But the Lancer memo isn't it."

"You're too clever for your own good. If I'm not after proof of the disinformation story, what *do* you think I'm up to?"

"I'm not certain. Our deal was that you were going to tell me. I held up my end. You're reneging."

"Impasse." Phillips shrugged.

"Pity," Michaelson said. "Well, when conceptual negotiations get bogged down, State Department doctrine is to try for incremental steps. I need the police report on Demarest's death. Do you think you can get it?"

"We're talking about *Maryland*," Phillips said. "For what I have in petty cash I could probably get the state seal and the cell phone number of the governor's mistress. But if I do, why should I share the thing with you?"

"Two reasons. First, if you get it to me by two o'clock tomorrow afternoon, I won't go after it through other sources. Second, I'll tell you something that will help you figure out how Demarest died."

"That's it?"

"Last, best, and final offer. Take it or leave it."

"What makes you think I give a damn about how Demarest died?"

Michaelson's face hardened and a splash of calculated cruelty colored his voice.

"Because I saw Willie and Project go after him."

Phillips didn't flinch and no flicker of emotion disturbed his features.

"Time will tell, then, won't it?" he said carelessly. "Why don't you run along now?"

"If you insist," Michaelson said, heading for the door. "I was rather hoping for a ride, though. I took a cab out here, and I'm getting a bit tired of this particular Metro trip."

"No can do. I am going to toss the place now."

"Why?" Michaelson asked.

"Because you missed something, you arrogant old fossil, that's why."

Thirteen

"What does the smoke changing color turn out to mean?" Michaelson shouted. He was shouting to make himself heard over the noise of water running in the bathroom sink as he shaved.

"It means an accelerant was used to start the fire," Marjorie yelled back from the small kitchen area in Michaelson's apartment. "Barbecue starter fluid or something like that. A fairly large amount, apparently."

As in many oversized villages, gossip is Washington's principal cultural activity. The difference is that in real villages the gossipers don't tend to get the facts quite as systematically and consistently wrong as the capital variety do.

Michaelson and Marjorie, for example, had known each other for just over thirty years. The first ten had combined intellectual intimacy with a carnal chastity that Sir Gawain himself could not have reproached, but Georgetown salons had routinely credited them with a decade of adulterous delight. Later, after a divorce each, they had found their way to each other's beds and to an unspoken understanding that they would not find their way to anybody else's. They had never lived together, shared incomes or credit cards, or registered at hotels under the same name. Indeed, the sex that complemented their relationship had never defined it, their frequent trysts representing one very pleasurable aspect of their couplehood but not its essential point. This comfortable fidelity had continued so long by the mid-nineties, however, that the same D.C. gossip that had once approved their sophisticated but imaginary adultery now shrugged disdainfully at what it assumed had become a stodgy, plain vanilla marriage.

Marjorie set sourdough English muffins slathered with margarine next to two cups of black coffee on the table.

"Between that datum about the color change and the Baggie that I cleverly remembered," she continued, automatically lowering her voice as the water stopped, "you may well have the highlights of the police report you're trying to sweat out of poor Avery."

"I'm hoping the report might also say something about cause of death," Michaelson said. He came into the kitchen with his unknotted bow tie hanging around his neck and his collar button unfastened. "Thank you for fixing breakfast."

"It was the least I could do after your hospitality," Marjorie said. "I thought of something else, by the way. When we were standing around in the yard, one of the firemen said something about the bedroom smoke detector not having batteries. That might be in the police report too."

"A bonus," Michaelson said as he tucked his unfurled napkin into his shirt. "In one sense, of course, the whole thing will be a bonus if Phillips chooses to produce it."

" 'Of course.' I love that. What are you talking about?"

"We could probably get the substance of the police report without any cooperation from Phillips," Michaelson said. "If nothing else, we could infer the bulk of it from the interrogation I'll undoubtedly undergo once the police find out I was poking aggressively around Demarest's home and office a short time before he died."

"Why are you muscling Phillips for it, then?" Marjorie asked.

"Because if he wants the information I promised in exchange badly enough to procure the report and give it to me, that will confirm my suspicion that he and Demarest were working together in some way on whatever the Calvert Manor project was."

"Confirm it how?"

"By showing that he cares about whether someone murdered Demarest and if so who it was. If Demarest was just an independent source or an unwitting tool, then Phillips would shrug off his death as a secondary issue—collateral damage. If Demarest's death bothers Phillips enough that he wants to look into it, that will tell me that they were collaborating. I've heard a lot of nasty things about Avery Phillips, but he takes care of his own people."

"Perhaps," Marjorie said thoughtfully as she added strawberry jam to the second half of her English muffin. "Or maybe it will just mean that explaining Demarest's death will help Phillips get what he's going after."

"I'm not sure," Michaelson said after a moment's reflection, "but I think we just said the same thing."

"Do you have any other ideas, in case nothing happens by two o'clock?"

"None very promising. There's C-Sharp. He probably won't talk to me. And there's Connaught the spook. Or ex-spook. He'll lie through his teeth. This could be challenging." Michaelson rose, dabbed at his lips with his napkin, and carried his dishes to the sink.

"Do you have any agenda between now and two?" Marjorie asked. "Or are you just tied up with your junior fellow?"

"My junior fellow is putting his paper through the word processor one more time. From the top. That appalling little note I put on it last week may be the four most productive lines I've written since I left the service. My main endeavor between now and two o'clock is going to be trying to see Jim Halliburton."

"You don't sound like you're looking forward to it," Marjorie said.

"I'm not."

Not quite a hundred minutes later Marjorie found enough of a respite in the midst of an uncharacteristically bustling morning at Cavalier Books to start thinking again about the plausibility of Michaelson's analysis.

She would have caught the allusion to Judge Jeffreys and the Bloody Assizes and the king-over-the-water toast if Michaelson had sprung them on her. True, she would have caught them because of countless hours in her misspent youth devoted to historical romances. But that was really the point, wasn't it? Anyone drawn without ulterior motive to an outfit like the Stuart Restoration Society would have something like that in her (or his) background. Richard was right: Demarest's interest in that organization had to have been some kind of cover.

But how far did that really get them? That didn't necessarily mean that Demarest was after some sinister document or gothic secret at Calvert Manor. He might have been as shallow as he seemed. Maybe he was just fortune hunting—maybe he was just after Catherine.

Catherine again. Every time she thought this through, Marjorie came back to Catherine. Whatever she might be, Catherine definitely wasn't shallow. If there was a single key to this entire puzzle, Marjorie thought, it wasn't hidden on some microfiche at the CIA; it was inside Catherine's head.

She replayed Michaelson's account of his talk with Demarest. The confrontation at the nightclub. The layout there, Demarest without even an office, just a lockable desk behind a partition. Demarest at the health club, fascinated by neither the boys nor the girls but the mirror. Then Phillips at Michaelson's flat, telling Michaelson he'd missed something.

She briskly straightened some papers on the counter, went to the phone, and dialed Michaelson's number. She got his voice mail, as she'd known she would.

"Give me a call if you can before you talk to Phillips," she said. "I just had a thought."

Though he was singing Gershwin and Porter, the man accompanying himself on the upright piano seemed to be trying for a ragtime look: sleeve garters, straw boater, that kind of thing. His audience gave no sign of resenting the anomaly. Gathered in a double semicircle of wheelchairs and folding chairs in the Extended Care Facility's dayroom, the eighteen elderly residents watched the performance without complaint, smiling, nodding, some of them making game attempts to sing along.

Michaelson spotted Jim Halliburton thirty feet away, at the other end of the room, in front of a flickering but silent television. He wore a blue plaid pajama top tucked into a pair of charcoal gray suit pants with the once-white waistband curling over the belt. His wheelchair occupied a rectangle of sunshine streaming through glass doors that looked out on a snow-covered patio. He was not smiling, nodding, or attempting to sing along.

Michaelson worked his way over to the older man, who glanced up at his approach. Limp white whiskers at least three days long stood out on each cheek against his sallow complexion. A class-reunion-type frown combining recognition and puzzlement creased his face when he got a good look at Michaelson, as if Halliburton dimly recalled him in context but couldn't remember his name.

"Good to see you again, Jim," Michaelson said as he came up and took a seat near Halliburton, careful not to block his view of the television. "Richard Michaelson."

"Of course," Halliburton said. "Michaelson. Near East/ South Asia. Good to be back where it's halfway warm again. It was colder than a by-God in Peshāwar, let me tell you."

Michaelson kept his expression carefully neutral. Peshāwar had once been an American air force base in what had once been West Pakistan on the front lines of what had once been the Cold War.

"Catching up on the news stateside," Halliburton said, nodding at the TV.

Following the nod, Michaelson saw closed-caption text crawling in white block letters through black rectangles at the bottom of the screen. The channel was MSNBC. The caption said that a U.S. official was having "frank and productive" discussions with his Chinese opposite number. Perhaps inspired by the Great Wall stock footage behind him, the commentator was predicting that most-favored-nation status for China would continue.

"Cozying up to the PRC," Halliburton said. "Has to be done, of course. But GOI isn't going to like it. Hope someone over there is thinking about that."

"GOI" is State Department argot for "Government of India." Although Halliburton's head-snap this time went toward the patio doors, beyond which lay nothing of more institutional importance than the Rockville Pizza Hut, Michaelson surmised that his reference to "over there" meant the White House.

"You're no doubt correct," Michaelson said. "But then

the last time we managed to please GOI was the arms sale back in 'sixty-two.''

"That *was* marvelous, wasn't it?" Halliburton responded with a flush of enthusiasm as his eyes sparkled. "Very rich. Nehru has always been such a self-righteous little prick. Loftily disdaining military aid—*until* Chinese Reds start pouring across the Kashmir border. Then all of a sudden it was 'Please, please, could we have some tanks thank you.' "

"I remember it well," Michaelson said, smiling warmly. He barely managed to squeeze these four words in between the cascading waves of Halliburton's continued reminiscence.

"That's just the way it is with them and we might as well get used to it," Halliburton said. "I remember a meeting with LBJ a while back when we were having a crisis with India every two months. This was during Indira Gandhi's first time around as prime minister. She's Nehru's daughter, you know."

"Yes," Michaelson said mildly.

"And we were sitting there in the White House basement getting instant wisdom from all these NSC whiz kids with their White Paper expertise. All of a sudden someone rushes in with a cable for the president. LBJ opens it and reads it, and this huge grin spreads over that enormous face of his. He crumples the cable up and squashes it in his fist, which he raises over his head. And he says, 'Gentlemen, we have that little lady right by the balls.' "

Halliburton threw himself back in the wheelchair with a delighted, wheezing laugh that continued until drool began to trickle from the corners of his mouth and stream down his chin. The laughter suddenly stopped and a stricken look came over Halliburton's face until Michaelson handed him a handkerchief so that he could mop the spittle up properly.

"Thank you," he said, as he recovered. "We can't over-react to this kind of aggravation, though. We have to remember that they're a democracy, and their politicians have to play to unlettered galleries, just like ours do."

This expatiation went on for several dozen more seconds, as Halliburton treated Michaelson like a callow FSO fresh from the Fletcher School and needing to be shaken out of his postwar American triumphalism. Well before it was finished, the China story on MSNBC had given way to an apparent rebroadcast of an appearance by Marcus Humphreys on a talk show the previous day. Michaelson's internal antennae quivered. He didn't flatter himself that his political savvy extended to electoral calculations, but he knew that when an ordinary congressman started showing up on TV and radio this regularly, there were important people who thought he might be more than a congressman before long.

Halliburton's *tour d'horizon* of elementary geopolitics finally wound down just as Humphreys was being asked about affirmative action. Humphreys was launching into what the captions suggested would be a provocative analogy between affirmative action and corporal punishment when Michaelson seized the opportunity to respond to Halliburton's exposition.

"Quit right," he said.

He examined Halliburton's eyes searchingly, but he wasn't looking for a miraculous flicker of lucidity. He didn't believe in miracles and he certainly wasn't expecting any here. Washington's rather tawdry present wasn't going to intrude into the destiny-shaping Johnson/Nixon/Kissinger world where Halliburton's mind had now comfortably planted him. Michaelson hadn't come to seek information but to convey some.

"You sent me a message just before you went to the hospital," he said, leaning forward.

"Yes," Halliburton said. Michaelson could tell from the older man's expression that this was an acknowledgment of Michaelson's statement, not a sign that Halliburton had the faintest idea of what he was talking about.

"I just wanted you to know that the situation has been appropriately taken care of."

"Excellent."

"Your concerns were well founded," Michaelson continued. "But the problem has been dealt with. Everything's under control."

"Is it now? Well, good, good. Knew I could count on you. Glad to hear it."

If someone had asked Michaelson what he thought he had accomplished by speaking these words, he would have evaded the question as diplomatically as he could. It was like jazz: If you had to ask, you wouldn't understand. It was what Marjorie would have called a small thing, done well.

"Is there anything else we can usefully discuss today?" Michaelson asked then.

"No, I can't say there is." Halliburton was now decisive, an all-business section chief wrapping up a staff meeting so busy people could get back to work. "This place is actually very convenient to the fudge factory, though, and you can drop by again if something comes up before I'm back at my desk."

"Until next time, then," Michaelson said.

His spirits hadn't risen much by the time he got to the pay phone in the lobby. The Extended Care Facility was about as convenient to Foggy Bottom as it was to the Pentagon. And he hadn't heard "fudge factory" as slang for the State Department since 1979.

A call to his office number and a familiar code-punch produced a recorded voice informing him that he had three new voice mail messages. The first was Marjorie's, which intrigued him. The second, from Phillips, reported that he might be running a bit late but promised he'd be at Michaelson's office without fail by three P.M. That one satisfied him. The third was considerably more detailed.

"Rich-ard Michaelson," it began with insurance salesman heartiness. "Corbin Connaught here. You probably don't know me. I don't know that we ever served together, but I certainly heard your name. Anyway, I'm an FSO alumnus now, just like you. Doing a little consulting, this and that, here and there. Calvert Manor turns out to be a topic of mutual interest. I'd appreciate it if you'd give me a call at your early convenience."

The voice continued with Connaught's number, but Michaelson didn't hear it. He had already punched the code that deleted the entire message.

Fourteen

C ause of death was blunt trauma to the back of the head," Phillips said as he languidly tossed a thick manila envelope onto Michaelson's desk. "They have a blood, tissue, and indentation match from a protruding fireplace stone in front of the grate, so they figure that's the source of the blunt trauma."

"Hard to disagree," Michaelson said.

Phillips was now standing with his hands loosely joined behind his back, just short of parade rest, offering Michaelson about one-eighth of his profile. Michaelson slit the envelope open and took out two substantial documents. He began speed-reading the first, which was headed FIRE MARSHAL—PRELIMINARY INVESTIGATIVE REPORT.

"I ended up getting that from a cop source instead of the fire marshal," Phillips said.

"Even though it's still officially a fire marshal investigation?" Michaelson asked.

"So far. The police apparently aren't ready to start throwing jurisdictional elbows yet. But they're keeping up to speed. They don't want to commit to homicide and then not be able to prove it, but if it starts to move that way, they'll grab it."

"Their reluctance is understandable," Michaelson said as he began flipping through diagrams and tables. "Hallway door locked from the inside. Connecting bathroom door ditto. Plus the trustee didn't see anyone go into or out of either room, and she says she was looking."

"And the only window was supposedly limited to a maximum opening of a little over three inches."

"No 'supposedly' about it," Michaelson said. "I can tell you from personal experience that that part is right."

"There are identifiable footprints on the roof over the porch, but they apparently belong to Demarest."

"Yes," Michaelson said. "He was shoveling off the roof. Someone else's footprints were in the snow in the yard, according to this, but they led away from the house. And anyway there are no marks from a ladder or anything you could boost yourself with anywhere in the snow around the house."

"No one heard a helicopter," Phillips continued, "and they make a lot of noise."

"Chimney?"

"An anorexic midget couldn't have hidden in it, much less gotten down it into the room."

"Secret passages or hidden panels?" Michaelson asked.
"No."

"In sum, then: no way for anyone who was in the room with Demarest when he died to get out after Demarest got conked."

"No *apparent* way," Phillips demurred. "You've identified the question, not the answer."

"Point taken," Michaelson said.

"That's where the other item I gave you comes in," Phillips said. "It's a transcript of the conference call, annotated in increments of twenty seconds. You'll see that the longest period of time between tape-recorded comments by any given participant is a little under five minutes. You getting the picture?"

"Vaguely," Michaelson said.

"Everyone we know of in the house was in the living room when Wilcox assigned rooms for the conference call. Everyone who then went upstairs, except Demarest himself, was in on the call. No one saw anyone go upstairs between the call starting and the alarm ringing—and believe me, Willie and Project were keeping their eyes open. There wasn't any phone in Demarest's room."

"Bingo," Michaelson said, glancing at Wilcox's second-story floor plan, which was attached to the report.

"Right," Phillips said. "It's not enough to figure out some clever way for someone to get into and out of the locked bedroom. We also have to explain how someone got upstairs without being noticed by any of the witnesses near both stairways. Or how somebody already upstairs got to the room, murdered Demarest, and got back to their phone in less than five minutes."

"What about the footprints and this unidentified person apparently running from the back of the house after the alarm sounded?"

"Could be one of the spongers who was there with C-Sharp. Heard sirens and decided to make himself scarce in case the county mounties suggested a whiz quiz."

"A what?" Michaelson demanded.

"Urine test for drugs."

"The report doesn't say that any of the spongers are unaccounted for."

"The others may be covering for him. The footprints lead into the backyard and then to the driveway. From there he could have recovered his nerve and rejoined the group in the front yard, or snuck out to the street in the general confusion and gotten away."

"The footprints are tantalizing," Michaelson said. "Remember the old wheeze where the murderer walks backward *to* the crime scene, leaving a trail apparently going away from it?"

"Hollywood twaddle," Phillips snapped. "Whoever made those tracks was running *away* from the house. Cops examining footprints can tell whether someone is running forward or feeling his way backward. Besides, even if you have the murderer approach the house this way, you still can't get him onto the porch roof, much less into Demarest's room."

"Very disconcerting," Michaelson said. "No one could have killed Demarest and yet he's dead. We have a junior fellow here at Brookings who's unfazed by logical contradiction. I'd ask his opinion but he's busy revising a paper on the euro. If the police aren't ready to call it homicide yet, what is your cop source's working theory on how the blunt trauma came about?"

"Accident. I believe the term of art is autoerotic misadventure."

"To each his own, I suppose," Michaelson said. "It's a bit hard for me to visualize, though."

"The hypothesis goes like this. Bent out of shape about his exclusion from Catherine's presence and from the conference call, Demarest decided to pass his time in genteel self-gratification. After he ensured his privacy, he made a fire but ineptly failed to open the damper. Not realizing his mistake at first, he then ingested a recreational pharmaceutical—Ecstasy, in case you're keeping track—and began pursuing the solitary vice while, for some reason, sitting with his back to the edge of the bed. This so absorbed his attention that he either didn't notice the room filling with smoke or chose to finish what he had started before doing anything about it. Climax, ecstatic physical spasm, backward reflex, tumbles off the bed, hits his noggin, lights out."

"I see," Michaelson said.

"I don't believe it either," Phillips said.

"Any pass by the constabulary at explaining the use of an accelerant on the fire?"

"That part of the theory is a bit lame. They say Cindy thinks maybe the firewood they used was pretreated with some kind of starter fluid. She apparently was rather vague about it."

"A conundrum," Michaelson said, drumming his fingers on the desk and gazing pensively out his window. "If this were a movie, of course, we could just pin it on the CIA."

"Here in the real world, unfortunately, no one is silly enough to think that a new corpse is less embarrassing than an old memo."

"Especially if the corpse has provocative associations."

"You're fishing without a license, Richard," Phillips said sharply, turning away from the wall and flinging himself a bit petulantly into the guest chair.

"Excuse me?" Michaelson asked mildly.

"The deal was, I get the police report, you give me something that would help me get to the bottom of Demarest's death. I've come across with the report plus a transcript of the conference call. So stop pumping me for information you think I have about Demarest's past, and deliver. C'mon, chop-chop, let's have it."

"Absolutely right," Michaelson said. He tossed Phillips a photocopy of the sentences he'd copied from Catherine Shepherd's notebooks.

"What's this?" Phillips asked.

Michaelson told him. Phillips spent a few seconds perusing the pages.

"Well, as kinks go this is pretty white-bread suburban.

In New York terms, it's a lot closer to dinner at La Nouvelle Justine than party time at a Chelsea leather bar."

"I defer to your undoubted expertise," Michaelson said.

"I won't deny that it's intriguing," Phillips said as he folded the photocopy into his inside coat pocket. "But you're holding out on me."

"You're mistaken," Michaelson said. "Indeed, you're projecting. You said I missed something at Demarest's apartment. You thought there was something interesting there besides the Lancer memo. You didn't find it when you searched the place, so you assume I found it and am keeping quiet about it. I didn't and I'm not."

"Hard for me to believe," Phillips said.

"And even harder for me to prove, since you probably know what this fascinating item is and I don't have the faintest idea."

Phillips made a face.

"Fortunately," Michaelson said, his own face brightening, "I do have an idea about where this thing is. Or, to be more precise, Marjorie has an idea on that subject."

"It's a good thing I'm not missing a performance of *Sunday in the Park with George* for this conversation," Phillips said with an exasperated sigh. "All right, I'll bite. Let's hear it."

Michaelson explained Marjorie's idea. Phillips's face remained impassive for two seconds after Michaelson had finished.

"Let's go," he said then.

It was about ten minutes after Phillips and Michaelson left Michaelson's office that Marjorie got a phone call from Carrie, the young woman who, when she wasn't busy earning her master's degree in library science, worked with generally unfailing reliability for Marjorie. Carrie explained that she was having a *Problem* and wouldn't be able to get in until half an hour past her scheduled starting time at four P.M.

Marjorie viewed this as providential. The commercial distractions generated by $327.98 in sales hadn't been nearly enough to divert her restless mind from the Calvert Manor puzzle. By midafternoon she had convinced herself that she had to talk to Catherine again. Doing that productively would require some information and resources that Carrie could gather more efficiently than she could.

"Actually," she said to her contrite employee, "we're not all that busy. Why don't you come in at five-fifteen, but do some things for me on the way?"

"Sure. What do you need?"

"Well, first, I'll need a large serving of cream of celery soup from Ellie's Deli, and a Thermos for it."

"Can do," Carrie said.

"Second, I need to know the date Andrew Shepherd died. It was a couple of years back, but it should have made the papers."

"Okaayyy," Carrie said, a bit dubiously.

"And what I'm particularly interested in," Marjorie concluded, realizing that she was about to complete Carrie's bafflement, "is what the weather was like that day."

Phillips didn't share Michaelson's taste for vigorous walks, so they took a cab to Club Chat Fouetté. The place was closed but Phillips (as Michaelson noted with interest) had a key, which he used on the front door. As they came in, he nodded at a solid-looking gent behind the bar, who nodded back without apparent interest or surprise.

"Demarest was a dummy owner for this and a couple of my other commercial properties," he explained to Michaelson during their brisk march toward the stage and the stairway. Then he raised his voice slightly, calling, "Where are you, Janos?"

"Right here," a voice shouted from their left.

The slightly built Eastern European who had let Michaelson in on his first visit surged at them from the hallway leading to the alley door. He came at Phillips with both fists flying.

Phillips pivoted, his arms cocked instantly in front of him. He absorbed a glancing left-fist punch on his upper right arm, then snapped his left arm up and out to block Janos's right jab. His own right fist darted out to smack Janos's temple. The blow sent Janos sprawling.

"Do your whimpering upstairs," Phillips said brusquely as he yanked the man to his feet. "That flooring cost nine thousand dollars, and salt water is bad for it."

He pushed Janos to the stairway, then nudged him up with a knee in the buttocks. Alternately massaging his wrist and the side of his face, Janos moved under his own power to what had been Demarest's desk and perched on top of it.

"You have to get over this Slavic sentimentality or Balkan or Magyar or whatever the hell it is," Phillips said to him. "If you'd tried that kind of nonsense with Project, he would've put you in the hospital."

Janos responded with the Anglo-Saxon obscenity customary under these circumstances, putting it in the imperative mood.

"That would be between me and Project, and a gentleman never tells," Phillips said. "Now. Please keep your mouth shut before I ask Mr. Michaelson here to avert his gaze long enough for me to shut it for you. You are to listen until told to speak. Got it?"

Janos salvaged what dignity he could with a second's deliberate delay, then nodded.

"Good. Three points. One. I didn't kill Preston. You think I did, but that's because you're a silly ass with less brains than the average desk jockey at Langley, and that's

112

saying something. Two. I want to find out who did kill Preston as much as you do. My reason is different than yours, but it's still a reason. Three. You are going to help me do it. Are we clear? Say yes."

"I don't believe you," Janos said. Michaelson felt a slight thrill of admiration at the courage it took for Janos to speak those four words.

"You don't *have* to believe me, you moron," Phillips snapped with unfeigned irritation. "You just have to be frightened enough to do exactly what I tell you."

Without waiting even an instant for reaction, Phillips then looked helplessly to heaven, stamped his foot, and walked around once in a very tight circle.

"Oh, very well, then," he said. "I'll explain it in terms simple enough for even you to wrap your tiny mind around."

Phillips stopped talking, closed his eyes, and took three deep breaths. In through the nose, out through the mouth. After the third breath, he opened his eyes. He waited another two or three seconds. Then he resumed speaking, all trace of aggravation gone.

"Preston wasn't trying to scam me," he said. "He may have let you believe he was because that's the kind of thing that would impress you, but he wasn't. Preston was trying to make a deal with me. He'd gotten something fair and square, and he wanted me to bid for it. There was no reason for me to be upset about that. Business as usual. Is this penetrating?"

His face impassive, Janos reached behind him and without looking found a four-pack of A&C Grenadiers at the back of the desk. Masking his continuing nervousness well but not perfectly, he took one of the cigars out, bit the tip off, and lit the cigar with a chartreuse Bic from his trouser pocket. Then, through a cloud of blue-gray smoke, handling the cigar with almost effete delicacy, he nodded.

"All right," Phillips continued. "Preston thought he had something very valuable. He did, but it wasn't what he thought he had. What he thought he had was basically worthless, and no one would give him the time of day for it."

"So you decided to screw him," Janos said.

"No, I decided to use him. There's a difference. I offered to let him work with me, and I offered him a generous cut if we brought it off. I didn't tell him what the deal was, because he didn't have to know. He was doing his part."

"Yes," Janos said evenly, nodding. "I should say he was *doing his part*. I should say he contributed, wouldn't you?"

"Precisely my point," Phillips said. "When he died, Preston Demarest was my soldier, doing my dirty work. I may be a cold-blooded, hard-nosed bastard, but I don't leave my people stranded on the embassy roof after the last helicopter takes off."

Janos puffed on the cigar without taking it out of his mouth, affecting diffidence. But Michaelson could see that his eyes changed.

"So what?" he said.

"So I want to know who killed him," Phillips said. "He had some assets in this little adventure that he didn't get from me. They weren't at his apartment. Finding them is the next step."

"If you think you're searching this desk," Janos said, "you're loco. You'll have to kill me first."

"It isn't in the desk. If it were, he wouldn't have walked out of here a few days before he died leaving my friend Michaelson standing unattended right next to the desk."

"Where are these mysterious assets, then?"

Phillips grinned at Janos's question. The bait was taken, the hook set.

"You're looking a little flaccid, Janos," Phillips said. "You need a workout. Let's go."

114

Fifteen

When Marjorie debriefed Michaelson about his excursion with Phillips and Janos to Bodies by Design, he attributed the success of their expedition to an important difference between the genders: Men look *less* dangerous naked than clothed.

Taking up most of the space in the men's locker room at Bodies by Design were full-sized lockers to store your street clothes in while you worked out. These were locked by keys. Janos had gotten a key to one for himself by showing his membership card, and keys for Phillips and Michaelson by asking for guest passes for them.

Lining the walls were six tiers of small, rectangular kit lockers, each one assigned to a member by name. Members used their kit lockers to hold their gym clothes, shoes, and toiletries between workouts. When a member finished running or pumping iron, he put his sweaty workout clothes into a mesh bag marked with the number of his kit locker. He threw this bag into a laundry bin. Over the next twenty-four hours, the mesh bags in the bins were supposed to go through a washer and a dryer before being returned to the appropriate kit lockers. Each kit locker had a combination lock, for the member assigned to it, and a key lock, for the attendants.

Which was why Michaelson, Phillips, and Janos found themselves standing in their birthday suits near the column of kit lockers that included, second from the bottom, one with the nameplate PRESTON DEMAREST. A white-shirted attendant a few yards off was working his way toward them, dumping bins at the head of each group of full-sized lockers into a large, wheeled laundry cart.

"Excuse me," Janos called to him. "My kit bag didn't make it back into my locker after my last time. Can we check some of these and see if it got in one of them by mistake?"

"Sure."

The attendant sidled toward Janos and opened the top locker on the Demarest column. Janos hoisted himself a bit to paw through the contents, accompanying his search with occasional grunts. The attendant paid desultory attention. What was Janos going to steal? A can of shaving cream? A jock strap?

"Nope," Janos said apologetically after several seconds.

They repeated the process with each of the kit lockers in the column, finally reaching Demarest's. With each iteration the attendant's impatience increased as his vigilance diminished. While Janos was going through Demarest's kit locker, Michaelson heard amidst the grunts something that sounded like "benes." The next thing he heard was Phillips's voice.

"Are you number thirteen thirty-seven?" Phillips called from two rows away.

"Sure am," Janos answered as both he and the attendant turned in Phillips's direction.

116

"They stuck it in mine," Phillips said, waving a mesh bag stuffed with gym clothes.

"What are the odds?" Janos commented to the attendant as he rose. "Thanks. Sorry for the trouble."

"No sweat," the attendant said.

He relocked Demarest's kit locker and returned to his laundry cart. Janos sauntered toward his full-sized locker, cradling the three-and-a-half-inch computer disk he had palmed from Demarest's kit locker.

"Nicely done," Phillips said in a low voice. "Now let's get dressed and back to the club so we can read the thing."

Michaelson reopened his locker and took out his underpants.

"Did you know it was a disk?" he asked.

"Couldn't be sure," Phillips answered.

"What if it had been an overstuffed, full-sized manila file folder?"

"The same basic trick would have worked. Might have needed a more aggressive diversion. But Janos is good at sleight of hand. Aren't you, you bitchy little peasant?"

This last comment was apparently intended to be good-natured. Janos greeted it with a dry laugh.

"Pending our actual look at the disk," Michaelson said then, "would you mind telling me what the thing is?"

"Unless Demarest was bluffing," Phillips said, "it's a complete patient history prepared by Catherine Shepherd's shrink."

"Looking back, it seems so frivolous to say that I met my fiancé because of something like the Stuart Restoration Society," Catherine said to Majorie around six-fifteen that evening. "Schoolgirlish. I'll never forget the Restoration Day high tea they had here. Serious with a capital *s*."

"I can imagine," Marjorie said after swallowing a silent spoonful of still-warm cream of celery soup.

"I remember one of the ladies—she must have been about seventy. She declaimed in perfect deadpan: 'Whigs stand for two principles: patriotism, by which they mean collaborating with a foreign invader; and religious liberty, by which they mean oppressing Catholics and Dissenters.' Everyone nodded, murmured approval, and sipped tea. It was absolutely priceless."

"It has been quite some time since I got very exercised about Whigs," Marjorie said. "But to be honest, I can see the appeal of a group like the Stuart Restoration Society. I have a friend who's a lobbyist for some outfit with 'hydraulic' in its name. Well into middle age, for no practical reason at all, he decided to become an expert on the Peloponnesian Wars. He said he just enjoyed reading about 'the forties' in books where that meant the period between 450 and 439 B.C."

"There was something like that about SRS," Catherine said. "Not just romantic, but romantically remote. But that's not why I fell for Preston; it was just what brought us together. Preston seemed to be there for me at exactly the moment I needed him, with exactly what I needed to have. This is delicious soup, by the way. Thank you so much for bringing it."

"You're very welcome. I had this silly image of you prostrate on a couch, wasting away from Victorian Women's Disease. I certainly wasn't prepared to find you hip-deep in estimates from contractors and applications for permits to repair the damage the smoke did to Calvert Manor."

"Intense activity has always been the best therapy for me. That's what brought me out of it . . . before." Catherine gave a few moments to an eye-clouded pause, then quickly resumed, her reflective tone giving way to bright chatter that sounded more forced with each sentence. "But I was telling you about Preston. I remember once, just after we

118

met, Cindy got it into her head to try to have baked Virginia ham ready for us when we got back from a matinee at the Kennedy Center. The minute we got in the house we could hear her in the kitchen, cussing up a storm. She had the ham out of the oven, *The Joy of Cooking* open on the counter, and she was standing over this ceramic bowl of something that looked like soggy bird feed."

"I can see where that might evoke some choice language," Marjorie said.

"And she was almost spitting at the bowl. 'This is supposed to be *glaze*, goddammit,' she was saying." Catherine's voice lowered to a whisper on the blasphemy, as if she were embarrassed at having the unladylike language pass her lips. " 'Bread crumbs, dry mustard, and cooking wine, just like this *worthless* book says, measured exactly right, and look at it.' And Preston said, very gently, 'I think it will make a marvelous glaze if you put it in a saucepan and heat it up for a few minutes.' "

Catherine threatened for a moment to dissolve in teary laughter at the image. After a couple of hiccups and eye dabs she continued.

"So Cindy goes, 'But it doesn't *say* anything about heating the stuff.' And Preston says, 'I know. That book is written by idiots.' After he heated it up, of course, the glaze was fine and the ham was delicious. I can't really say why, but that kind of thing just seemed very special to me."

The last comment brought real tears, streaming down Catherine's cheeks in anguish rather than laughter. Marjorie kept her mouth shut, limiting herself to a squeeze on Catherine's arm while the minisobs ran their course. She wasn't in any hurry. She wasn't here to pump Catherine about what "before" was all about. She already knew. While she drove to Calvert Manor Michaelson had called her and hit the highlights of the shrink's report—including the intriguing fact that Catherine hadn't started seeing the psychiatrist after her father's suicide but several years before her father had died.

"I can certainly understand why Preston appealed to you," Marjorie said gently when Catherine had herself back under control. "He'd appeal to most healthy young women. In the short time since I met you, in fact, I haven't been able to figure out why Cindy treated him so disdainfully."

"Cindy has a tendency to behave as if she wants Alicia Silverstone to star in the movie version of her life. You know, rebellious brat from central casting. That's part of it. But also, I think she really felt Preston wasn't right for me."

"As a fully emancipated adult legally entitled to own property, sign contracts, and consume alcoholic beverages in public," Majorie said, "wouldn't that be sort of your business?"

"Try explaining that to Cindy," Catherine said. "Ever since Mom dropped out of the picture, Cindy has treated me like she was the big sister. I mean, she was smoking in eighth grade, but when I started flirting with Marlboro Lights my senior year in high school, she suddenly got religion and turned into the surgeon general on me. You know, stealing packs from my purse to throw them away and that kind of thing. That's what that health Nazi crack I made the first time we met was all about. And when someone offered me a joint at a party one night she went absolutely postal. Gave him an elbow right in the kidneys. She was an interscholastic gymnast, so that elbow had to mean some serious pain."

"It seems a little fanatical," Marjorie said.

"It also seems a little ironic, given the controlled substances C-Sharp is into," Catherine said dryly. "I remember once Dad was out of town, which he was a lot, and I was planning on going to a kegger that weekend. I mean,

120

I was *seventeen*. Cindy found out there weren't going to be any adults there. So that night she faked these horrible stomach cramps and fever so I'd have to stay home with her instead of going. And the next morning I found out the cops raided the party and busted almost everyone there for beer and pot."

"She sounds extremely protective," Marjorie said. Carefully.

"She sounds controlling," Catherine said. "And I guess she has been. It would have been nice to make my own mistakes. But she means well. She felt I needed that kind of protection because of . . . some things that happened."

Several seconds of silence followed while Catherine appeared to concentrate intensely on her soup.

"I'm sorry about these vague allusions I keep making," she said then vacantly. "It's terribly impolite. And I'm making it sound so gothic, like I spent my junior high years decapitating house cats or something, when it's nothing like that at all."

Marjorie choked back an instant's panic as she saw Catherine shaking her head quickly and snatching with her right hand at imaginary specks on her cheek.

"What I've always found, actually," Marjorie said, using a conversational tone as if she were discussing the merits of different china patterns, "is that what we're most reluctant to discuss isn't the conventionally or traditionally shocking things. The things we have the most terrible need to keep private are those that are awful for reasons only we fully understand."

Catherine's head stopped shaking and her eyes fixed on Marjorie's as an intrigued expression slipped over her face.

"I'm not sure I understand what you mean," she prompted.

"I'll give you an example," Marjorie said after a deep breath. "I'm going to tell you something only two other people in the world know: the reason I divorced my husband."

Catherine demurred, but the guiltily fascinated glint in her eyes said that the protest was mostly for form.

"I divorced him after thirteen years of marriage because he slapped me in public. Not because he slapped me, but because he slapped me over Amaretto after a formal dinner party in the home of a family that had known mine for three generations."

"Oh, my word," Catherine gasped, ingenuously covering her mouth with her right hand.

"He was very clever with words, and quite aggressive verbally. He made his living being that way. That particular night he apparently felt like offending everyone in the room. He said you could either elect Democrats and have incompetents in office or elect Republicans and have criminals. I'd had about enough of his mood, so I said, 'Yes, or we could elect the guy you backed last time and have both.'"

"Oops," Catherine said.

"'Oops' is right. He didn't lash out in anger. He looked at me quite coolly for two full seconds. Then he lifted his arm and gave me a sharp little palm smack right across the chops."

"How awful," Catherine said, shaking her head deliberately.

"He'd slapped me a couple of times before," Marjorie said, "as I had him, to be fair. But those had been at home, when we were by ourselves, having the kind of fights well-bred couples have now and then. Not that that's okay, but it happens. This was different."

"Of course," Catherine said.

"When he slapped me in front of people we both knew," Marjorie continued, "he was degrading me. Literally. He was lowering my rank in the only world that was important to me then. He was trashing things that gave meaning and value to my way of life—the standards and values that define a particular kind of life. He wasn't just hitting me, he was rejecting me, and demanding that I reject myself. And he knew it."

Catherine reached out tentatively to touch Marjorie's hand.

"Aside from me and now you," Marjorie said, "the only people who know that that's why I divorced him are the ex himself and Richard Michaelson. Most people I know would be appalled to think that I'd view a public slap as fatal to our marriage when I'd shrugged off occasional private ones—that appearances and public status were so essential to me. So I've mostly kept it to myself. Until now."

Catherine withdrew her hand and gazed searchingly at Marjorie.

"You told me this to show me you understand, I see that," she said. "And I think you do understand. But you're doing more than that, aren't you? You're giving me permission. Permission to dump my own past on you."

"Or not, as you like," Marjorie said. "After all, isn't permission what you were seeking with those vague allusions you reproached yourself for?"

"I'm sorry," Catherine said a bit petulantly as she snapped her head away from Marjorie. "I'm not used to being so transparent."

"I'm not Cindy," Marjorie said. "I'm not going to make decisions for your own good and cram them down your throat. If you want to talk, I'm here. If you'd rather not, there's no one in the world who'd understand better than I."

Catherine sat quite still for a second or so. Then she pushed the soup bowl aside and began rummaging with frantic intensity through papers and notes spread over the dining-room table. When she spoke again the words came tumbling out, rapid-fire at first and then accelerating.

"Darn it, I knew I'd left one of the estimates upstairs. I'm being a terrible hostess. Could-you-excuse-me-one-minute-please?"

Without waiting for a response, she bolted from the dining-room table and raced upstairs. Marjorie stayed where she was. A woman is entitled to cry in private if she wants to.

She wasn't sure, later, how long she sat there. Five minutes in a strange, silent house can be an eon, ten minutes an eternity. When she eventually did move, it wasn't because she lost patience. At some point her gut just told her that something was wrong. She rose deliberately from the table and began quietly climbing the stairs toward the dark hallway above her.

She found Catherine in the first place she looked: the guest room where Demarest had died. Catherine sat on the floor in the dark bedroom, staring at fireplace stones that glinted in pale winter moonlight.

"It's funny," Catherine said without turning around as soon as she'd had some time to sense Marjorie's presence. "I feel that I know you as well as I know anyone, even though I'd never met you until a short time ago. I've felt you understood things from the first time we met. About this house, and my father. And me. I've felt I could talk to you about things, the way I wish I could talk to my mother. I suppose a shrink would say that's why I was asking permission, as you put it, dropping all those soap opera hints, subconsciously hoping that you'd draw me out so I could unload on you."

"I'm very glad you feel that way. But you don't owe me a thing. You don't have to tell me anything you'd rather keep to yourself."

"This is where I found them," Catherine said dully, turning her gaze back to the fireplace.

Marjorie braced herself. From Michaelson's summary she had a pretty good idea about what was coming, and she wasn't looking forward to it. But there was no leaving now. When you've brought someone this far, you see the thing through.

"A few years after Mom and Dad were divorced," Catherine said, her voice now small and far off, "Cindy and I were in different schools with different vacation schedules for two semesters. Cindy was spending her spring vacation with Mom, and mine didn't start for a week. I was supposed to be on this weekend debate trip, to Richmond. But my partner got sick Friday afternoon, during the second round. So we couldn't go on, and one of the parents drove us both back. I didn't even think to call Dad. I just waltzed into the house without warning, right before midnight. My partner had given me some pot to hide for her so her parents wouldn't find it. I snuck up to this room because it wasn't used much and I figured this was a good place to stash it until I could get it back to her. I didn't even think about smoking it myself."

Catherine shook her head and smiled briefly at this fastidious, honor student nuance. Then, offering Marjorie a now grimly self-mocking smile, she continued.

"And here they were. I walked in on my father doing a Clinton. Except with another man."

At the last four words a quaintly bashful phrase from Stuart-era English law flooded unbidden into Marjorie's memory: "The abominable and detestable crime against nature not to be named among Christians."

"Dear Lord," she murmured.

"That was quite a jolt, as you can imagine. But that wasn't the worst part."

Abruptly, Catherine rose to her feet, walked toward the door, and flipped on the overhead light. She strolled around the room, touching the bed, the lamp, the window.

Her meanderings finally brought her to the bathroom door, where she fingered the ancient snap bolt. Turned the release knob to retract the bolt into its housing. Let go of the knob and watched the bolt shoot out. Swung the door shut and watched the bolt bounce off the newly repaired bracket, keeping the door from closing. Retracted the bolt again and pushed the catch up. Let go of the release knob and watched the bolt stay in place, inside the housing. Slammed the door shut as hard as she could. Trying to jar the bolt loose? Marjorie wondered. If so, she failed. Then, with a shrug, she pushed the catch back down. The bolt shot out of its housing into the bracket, locking the door.

"Preston had to have locked himself in, didn't he?" she said, her voice suggesting oddly detached and clinical interest. "There isn't any other way, is there?"

"It certainly looks that way," Marjorie agreed.

"He wanted to make sure I didn't see him by accident, the way I had my father." Just as suddenly as she'd broken off her previous train of thought, Catherine straightened, squared her shoulders, and whirled to face Marjorie. When she resumed speaking her tone had become almost accusatory. "The worst thing was this. The man kneeling in front of Dad like some White House intern in her presidential knee pads looked kind of like a male version of me. It was spooky. I mean, not a fraternal twin or anything like that, just a kind of resemblance in build and looks and movement. As if he'd gone to a lot of trouble to make himself look like me. He was wearing a girl's National Cathedral School uniform. He even had on a wig the same color as my hair, and cut about the same way."

Catherine held Marjorie's eyes and gazed at her with an intense directness that nearly made Marjorie recoil.

"And so I knew what Dad really wanted. Me. All the time. All those years. And I felt so incredibly guilty. I was like, my parents are divorced, and that's my fault. My father's a pervert, and that's my fault. God knows what my mother is, but whatever it is that's my fault too."

Marjorie reached out to grip Catherine's arms but found herself embracing air. Moaning softly in between dry gasps, Catherine had collapsed on the floor, knees tucked under her breasts and arms wrapped around her knees.

Marjorie glanced urgently around the room. No phone. Of course, that was the point of sending Demarest to this room the day of the auction. She hustled to the hall and into the sewing room next door, praying for a phone as she scurried. She spotted one on a table by the window and hurried over to it. She had just lifted the receiver when she heard a louder wail from the room she'd just left. Still gripping the receiver, she stepped quickly back toward the door. The receiver's connecting cord was long, but she ran out of slack about a foot short of the door. She threw the receiver impatiently to the floor and then almost bowled Catherine over as she ran back through the guest room doorway.

"It's okay," Catherine said, very stiff-upper-lippish all of a sudden. "Sorry about that. I'm all right now."

"I don't think so," Marjorie said.

"No, really. I just had to get that out."

"When did Cindy find out?" Marjorie asked, keeping an edgy eye on Catherine.

"That summer for sure. Maybe earlier. She was a very bright kid."

"I don't know if it helps," Marjorie said. "But I think she blames herself for not finding your father's body before you did. I've taken a couple of logical leaps, but I think she feels she should have gotten here before you did that day."

"That's exactly the kind of thing she would think." Catherine turned away then, shaking her head in the familiar self-critical way. "I'm sorry. I can't believe I inflicted this on you."

Marjorie leaned forward and hugged the young woman as if she were a small girl who'd woken up shaking and sobbing from a nightmare.

"Please stop apologizing," she said in gentle reprimand. "I'm very touched that you chose to trust me with this, and I'm grateful to have shared it with you."

Then, at last, to Marjorie's vast relief, a cascade of healthy, cleansing tears finally came from Catherine.

As she drove back to Washington late that night, Marjorie thought about Preston Demarest. A lot. She thought about him choosing the ensemble he'd wear when he first approached Catherine; checking his hair to make sure he'd gotten every blazing copper strand in place; reviewing the briefing book someone had given him on the Stuart Restoration Society; glancing once more at the shrink's notes; and driving confidently out to Calvert Manor, knowing every scintilla of the searingly personal story Catherine had just recited, and planning exactly what buttons he was going to push and how he was going to push them; thinking about how he was going to use her; how he was going to manipulate her; how he was going to hurt her; and feeling his loins stir with excitement at the prospect.

Whoever killed him, Marjorie thought fiercely to herself, I'm glad he's dead. God damn him to hell.

Sixteen

So the next step is to talk to C-Sharp?" Marjorie asked the following morning after she and Michaelson had exchanged telephonic accounts of the previous day's escapades.

"That's the plan. Phillips has agreed to try it at Club Chat Fouetté early this evening, when the band shows up to get ready for its performance tonight."

"It couldn't have been easy to talk him into that."

"Best piece of negotiating I've done since I convinced you to try falafel," Michaelson said.

"I'm sure you had your reasons, but I can see Phillips's point. It sounds like a pretty complicated way to interview someone."

"I want this to be an interview, not an interrogation," Michaelson said. "Phillips has an occasional penchant for excessive enthusiasm. I thought it best to arrange for witnesses."

"Fair enough," Marjorie said. "Please let me know what happens. I'll be passing my time running a bookstore and meeting a payroll. Do you have anything on your agenda between now and the rendezvous this evening?"

"I thought that all I had was a two o'clock symposium at Georgetown on the euro. During our conversation, however, the message-waiting light on my phone has come on, so my day may be filling up."

"Let's hope mine does. Ciao."

The message was from Connaught. His unctuous recorded voice covered the same basic ground he had gone over before, sounding a bit hurt that Michaelson hadn't returned his call. This time Michaelson wrote Connaught's number down when he gave it. Over the past sixteen hours his interest in talking to the gentleman had increased considerably.

He reached Connaught's voice mail when he called back. He kept his voice neutral to chilly as he recorded his own message.

"Richard Michaelson," he said. "I can see you in my office between twelve-fifteen and twelve forty-five this afternoon. The receptionist will buzz someone to show you back."

With plenty of time remaining before the arbitrary deadline he'd just given Connaught, Michaelson pulled out the investigative report on Demarest's death that he'd gotten from Phillips. He folded it over to the thick packet of appendices.

Appendix A was the Calvert Manor floor plan that Wilcox had marked to show where the various conference call participants should park themselves. For seven minutes he studied page one, covering the first floor. He left his mind blank, letting the information flow in unfiltered. He did the same thing, but for twice as long, with the schematic for the second floor.

He continued this process through the remaining items in the appendices: the list of people on the conference call and the numbers for the telephones they had used; a photocopied page from a book, broken up by equations and chemical formulas, with text explaining how to compute the rate of carbon dioxide buildup in the bloodstream induced by smoke inhalation; an inventory headed TAGGED AND BAGGED, listing everything the police had taken from Calvert Manor as evidence; copies of the written purchase offers that had been submitted for Calvert Manor at the time of the conference call; and a list of everyone known to have been on the property when the conference call started, with indications of where they were, which ones had been interviewed, and which ones hadn't.

Prominent among the latter, of course, being Richard Michaelson, who still hadn't been contacted. Which, the more he thought about it, was rather interesting. If any investigation worthy of the name was going on, why hadn't anyone talked to him by now? If the investigation had effectively stopped, why? Or, more important, who had stopped it?

He turned back to the list of conference call participants. No surprises. Wilcox, Catherine, Cindy, Marjorie, and Willie, all on extensions using the phone number for Calvert Manor. Phillips at what the phone book verified was his office number. And Patrice Helmsing and Shepherd *mère* at numbers with exotic area codes.

He flipped to the two closely typed pages of the Tagged and Bagged section. Once again, nothing particularly striking: logs from the fireplace, fiber samples, a partial cast of the stonework in front of the fireplace, the Baggie that Marjorie had mentioned to him. The cover for the smoke detector in the guest room where Demarest had died. The clothes Demarest had been wearing. And, apparently, some clothes he hadn't been wearing:

GYM BAG, 1 (NIKE), VINYL, ZIPPERED

Contents: Running shorts, 1 pr. (men's L, Russell), n/blue; T-shirt, 1 (men's L, Nike), yellow;

jockstrap, 1 (L, Bike); running shoes, 1 pr. (men's 10½, Nike Air), white w/black trim; tube socks, 1 pr. (knee length, Wigwam); street shoes, 1 pr. (men's 10½, Rockport), dark brown; sweatpants, 1 pr. (men's L, Russell), royal blue; hooded sweatshirt, 1 (men's L, Russell), royal blue.

Michaelson turned back to the text of the report and scanned through it until he found a sentence fragment mentioning that the police had found the gym bag in Demarest's car.

Locking the report away again, Michaelson glanced at his watch. Almost eleven-fifteen. Two floors down from his office and seven minutes later, he found a nook where a young woman gazed serenely at a computer screen from beneath no-nonsense brown bangs and behind no-nonsense glasses with black plastic frames.

"Good morning, Ms. Dennison," he said.

"Good morning, Mr. Michaelson," she said warily, her eyes still fixed on the screen. "Did you decide you'd like some visuals for your Georgetown presentation after all?"

"Oh no, nothing like that. For that kind of thing I wouldn't change my mind on two hours' notice."

Leaning back in her steno chair, she folded her arms across her chest and looked up at him with undisguised skepticism.

"A one-eighty on minuscule notice wouldn't exactly set a precedent around here," she said. "What can I do for you?"

"You can answer a question, I hope," he said. "Is it possible to take part in a centrally controlled conference call on a cordless phone, without anyone else knowing?"

" 'Centrally controlled.' Like with an AT&T conference operator and so forth?"

"Yes. Specifically, could you be joined to the conference on a conventional phone and then somehow dial your own digital phone number and continue with the call on that phone?"

"Not without letting AT&T in on it," Dennison said after a moment's thought. "They know every number that's in on the call because they charge for every number. The same electrical impulses that you'd make to connect your digital phone would tell AT&T's computer that you'd connected it. If one of the numbers already dialed had multiple extensions, you could pick up one of the extensions without tipping any computers off, but not an entirely new phone with a new number, cordless or not."

"I've seen something advertised on television where a call to your office number automatically bounces to your home number and then your digital phone number. Would that work on a conference call?"

"Sure. But AT&T would pick up the bounces, and their records would show all three numbers."

"Thank you very much," Michaelson said.

Corbin James Connaught was only about fifteen pounds overweight, but the way he moved combined with the arrangement of his extra baggage to create an impression of striking corpulence. He waddled into Michaelson's office and settled heavily into the guest chair that Michaelson indicated. His sallow complexion emphasized puffy cheeks and saclike jowls. The first thing he did on sitting down was unbutton his suit coat. He seemed to wedge himself right hip first into the chair, so that he could brace his right forearm against the top of the chair back. He dispensed with amenities, which was fine with Michaelson.

"I think you know what I want," he said.

"What I don't know is how badly you want it," said

Michaelson, who wasn't at all sure what Connaught wanted.

"I'm not going to kid you. I'm way down the food chain. Data security and opposition research. I can't guarantee the kind of thing you're after. Money I could do, but I expect that's not where your interests lie."

"Fair enough," Michaelson said, shrugging noncommittally.

"But if you deliver you have a place at the table," Connaught said. His eyes gleamed and his teeth showed in a passable smile as he spoke the last four words. "Not because I give you one but simply because you will have delivered. And because of where we are in the process. You'd be getting in very early."

"That's a little thin considering the risks, don't you think?" Michaelson asked, bluffing ferociously. "After all, the last chap you sent after this material ended up in the morgue."

Connaught didn't bother pretending to be baffled or astonished by this comment.

"Demarest wasn't our boy," he said flatly. "He shopped what he had to us after he got it, but that doesn't put us in a very exclusive club. He did everything but advertise the stuff in the classified section of the *Post*. But we didn't send him after it."

"Right," Michaelson said. "And I suppose he got the psychiatric report from the Library of Congress."

"I don't know what report you're talking about," Connaught said. "But if he got a confidential report and I had to guess where, my guess would be the same as yours."

Michaelson decided that Connaught wouldn't have anyone in this year's Oscar competition looking over his shoulder. Before speaking again, he briskly reviewed the relevant data he had. Marjorie might look at Cindy's uncharacteristically intense reaction to traffic-snarling snow,

134

note that Andrew Shepherd had killed himself on a snowy day, and feel that she had a sneak peak into Cindy's psyche. Michaelson didn't swing quite that freely in the psychological realm, but when it came to bureaucratic behavior, even a few pieces of hard evidence could provoke equally aggressive inferences from him.

Andrew Shepherd had given trip reports to Aldrich Ames at the CIA. Andrew Shepherd lived at Calvert Manor. Preston Demarest knew about the trip reports and, without being a rocket scientist, had somehow gotten the idea they were important. And, critically, he hadn't made the Andrew Shepherd/Calvert Manor connection on his own. Someone had told him about it, and prepared him well to pursue it.

"Help me to be certain that I'm clear on something, please," Michaelson said after the four seconds that it took to run over this information. He leaned forward to plant his elbows on his desk, and his words became a little more clipped than usual. "I mention a psychiatric report and you act as if I'm talking Greek. Are you seriously asking me to believe that you personally had nothing to do with the Central Intelligence Agency sending someone to seduce Andrew Shepherd when the Aldrich Ames scandal was about to go public?"

"That was years ago," Connaught protested, squeaking a bit near the end of the sentence. "Langley didn't need any shrink's notes to know that Shepherd swung with an occasional swish after his divorce. His predisposition was no secret, and once he got to be middle aged with thinning hair and a sausage gut, he was flattered by the attention of handsome young men. Not exactly a scoop. You're confusing two completely different episodes."

"Then please unconfuse me."

Michaelson leaned back and folded his arms across his chest, treating Connaught as if he were a junior subordinate trying to bluff his way through a report without thoroughly knowing the file. A typical Washington reaction to this attitude is to start displaying how much you know. Connaught responded with Pavlovian predictability.

"When Ames was about to blow," Connaught said with an exasperated sigh, "of course we checked to see if his contacts had kept any souvenirs. The kind of thing the director should know about before *The New York Times* did."

"Especially contacts like Shepherd, whom you'd used to give false information to Ames," Michaelson said.

"Well, *duh*," Connaught shot back. "You've been reading John le Carré again, haven't you?"

"That's the part I'd figured out all by myself," Michaelson said. "Tell me about the episode I've confused it with."

"After I left the agency, and well after Ames was old news, Demarest started telling anyone who could write a check that he could supply some hot information from Calvert Manor. I was working for the national committee by then and the committee wasn't interested. Demarest must have found someone who was interested because he apparently went back in. But it wasn't us."

"You mean the national committee wasn't interested until you found out Avery Phillips was," Michaelson said.

"That's the whole point," Connaught rejoined. "I'm deeply interested in what Phillips is after, which is emphatically *not* what Demarest was peddling on his own. That's what I want from you, and I want it before Phillips gets it."

"And you want it on spec."

"Can't be helped. I could tell you that if you come through, NSC or State is yours, but I'd be lying and you'd know it. All I can offer is good faith and no guarantees."

"That's what Jim Halliburton had, isn't it?" Michaelson

136

asked in a very quiet voice. "Good faith and no guarantees."

Connaught snapped his head in a quick, angry shake.

"I'm not taking the rap for that," he said with feral petulance. "The stakes were high. He knew what he was getting into."

"Yes," Michaelson said. "When a policy has been crafted by State Department professionals, legislated by Congress, and paid at least lip service by the White House, the risks associated with deliberately subverting it are indeed high. What Halliburton couldn't know was that the people who convinced him that the fate of the republic depended on such subversion would abandon him the first time things got a little hot."

"I know you'll go to your grave convinced that the bad guys on that are across the river, but you've got the wrong target. The critical leaks came from Foggy Bottom, not Langley. Jim Halliburton went down because an alumnus from your own shop sniffed out the money, followed the paper trail, and then goosed Congress into making a stink about it."

"I was talking about support, not exposure."

"If there's no exposure, you don't need support. Langley ran for cover and left Halliburton hanging. Fine, not our most heroic moment. But without the leaker, there wouldn't have been anything to run from. No scandal, no feeding frenzy in the media, no congressional hearings, no special prosecutor. Whoever leaked that story is the guy you ought to be saving all this festering resentment for."

"Thank you for your candor," Michaelson said with finality. "You've made your position clear. I know where to reach you."

After seeing Connaught out, Michaelson returned to his office and began filling his briefcase with materials he'd need for this afternoon's symposium. He brought a bit more vehemence than was customary to this process. There were two reasons for his irritation.

First, he'd been wrong about Connaught. He had assumed that Connaught was still working for the CIA and that his ostensible position with one of the political parties was a none-too-convincing cover. He now thought it plain that Connaught was doing exactly what he claimed to be doing. Whatever it was Connaught wanted, there was no earthly reason for the CIA to give two hoots about it. Besides, if Connaught had still been getting his checks from spook central, he could credibly have offered Michaelson bribes far more tangible than a vaguely limned place at the table.

The second reason was that, without realizing it, Connaught had fingered him. Connaught apparently didn't know that Michaelson was the State Department alumnus whose covert bureaucratic action had saved an element of Near Eastern foreign policy at the cost of destroying Jim Halliburton's career. And in some strange way, that just made it worse.

Seventeen

A new PRETTY GIRLS SMOKING CIGARETTES T-shirt complemented C-Sharp's desert camouflage pants and combat boots as he climbed to the mezzanine at Club Chat Fouetté that evening. He moved toward Phillips, who was gathered in a group with Michaelson, Willie, and Project near the railing that overlooked the stage below.

The nightspot showed considerably more life than it had on Michaelson's first visit. Waiters wearing white cowboy hats and black leather pants with nothing in between scurried among a handful of early patrons. Two techies in work clothes were on ladders, hanging crimson leather straps in the shape of the AIDS awareness symbol from fishing line strung over the small stage.

"Hey, Ageless," C-Sharp said affably. "Janos said you wanted to see me. What's happening?"

Phillips raised one eyebrow as he turned toward C-Sharp.

"Willie," he said, "C-Sharp wants to know what's happening. What's happening?"

"Charlotte Brontë jokes," Willie said solemnly. "Like, what brand of cooling equipment did Rochester use?"

"I give up," Phillips said.

"Jane Air. Who did Rochester leave his money to?"

"Jane Heir?"

"Right," Willie affirmed with a vigorous nod.

"Uh, guys?" C-Sharp said. "Hello?"

"Oh, I have one," Phillips said. "How did Rochester explain the mistake with Cheetah the monkey?"

"Jane Err?" Willie guessed.

"Bingo," Phillips said.

"Oooh-kayyy," C-Sharp said. "See ya."

"Don't you have a riddle for us, C-Sharp?" Phillips asked.

C-Sharp looked back over his shoulder.

"No," he said, with a thin, I-don't-like-this-game smile.

"Then we'll change genres," Phillips said. "Something contemporary. Let's see. Here's one for you: What happened at Calvert Manor in very early February, a few weeks ago?"

"I don't have the faintest idea. And I have a set in about seventy-five minutes with no sound check done yet."

He completed his original pivot but found Project in between him and the stairs. After a moment's aggravated indecision he whirled around to confront Phillips.

"Okay," he snapped. "What's going on?"

"I think you do know," Phillips said in a cajoling tone. "You just have to put your mind to it."

C-Sharp raised his hands palms out to chest level in a placating gesture.

"Look, guys. Here it is. I have no clue. No clue. Got it?"

"It would have been something fairly dramatic," Phillips said. "Something that would get your attention when it happened and stick in your memory afterward. Something involving Catherine Shepherd. Something that made her feel naughty and caused her to write a pietistic punishment sentence five hundred times on February third."

"I wasn't living there, okay?"

"You were doing other things there. On a regular basis."

The four-man semicircle arching around C-Sharp got a little tighter. C-Sharp's eyes swept the group as he gulped a quick breath through his mouth. He backed up until his hips brushed the top of the mezzanine railing. At the instant of contact he sketched a panicky jump forward as if he'd been shocked. Although Phillips, the nearest, was still several feet away, sweat popped out on C-Sharp's forehead and upper lip. A palsied shake took over his left hand.

"Something dramatic involving Catherine," Phillips repeated soothingly. "Something you didn't mention to the police. Just tell us, and then you can go play with your friends."

"I don't know dates, I can't—"

"Don't worry about dates. You know what we're talking about, don't you, C-Sharp? He knows, doesn't he, Willie?"

"He knows."

"Tell us, C-Sharp."

Eyes squeezed tightly shut, C-Sharp brought clenched fists up above his shoulders and then pumped his forearms back to his sides, like a true believer doing isometrics.

"The only thing I can think of," he said, "was this one night when I guess she and Preston had a fight."

"What did they fight about?" Phillips demanded.

"I don't know. It was upstairs. I was in the kitchen. I had the munchies."

"There's a surprise," Willie muttered.

"I heard raised voices, but sounding like people do when they're trying not to raise their voices. Then Preston

141

comes slamming downstairs and crashes out the back door."

"What time?" Phillips asked.

"Say not quite three A.M. We'd gotten back from a gig maybe half an hour before."

"Where was Cindy?"

"She had crashed."

"Continue," Phillips said. "Keep going till you hear the applause."

"Okay," C-Sharp said, accompanying the comment with a long, weary exhalation of breath. "Maybe ten minutes later there is this un*godly* scream from upstairs. 'PRESSS-TONNN!!!' I mean it cleared my sinuses out, man."

"Catherine?"

"Yeah."

"Uh-huh. Don't stop."

"She comes racing downstairs in a robe and nightgown. Before I know it she's out the door. Screaming all the way. Cindy's at the top of the stairs yelling. 'Don't let her run around out there alone! Stay with her!' So I hustle out and spot Catherine going into the garage. I follow her in. Garage door is closed and the lights are out till I turn one on. There's an engine running and I can smell exhaust. And there's Preston."

"Where's Preston?" Phillips asked impatiently.

"Behind the wheel in Cathy's car. Engine turned on, like I said. Staring through the windshield like a zombie. I was freaked, man."

" 'Like a zombie'?" Phillips said to Michaelson, shaking his head sadly. "The last pop music composer with a decent sense of simile was Neil Sedaka."

"Anyway," C-Sharp said, "Catherine pulls the car door open and throws herself on Preston. She's sobbing. She's sorry she's sorry she's sorry, oh-Preston-Preston-Preston, yatta-yatta-yatta, the usual chick-shit, y'know. So Preston

142

melts and they eventually go back inside all over each other. I was 'bout ready to puke."

C-Sharp stopped talking and looked around hopefully at the faces confronting him.

"Oh, what a shame," Phillips said, shaking his head theatrically in hammy disappointment. "And you were doing so well, too. Wasn't he doing well, Willie?"

"Real well," Willie said. "We were all proud of you, C-Sharp."

"Yeah," C-Sharp said. "Okay. That's it. Gotta go."

"Not yet," Phillips said as Project again intercepted C-Sharp. "You see, I think you left something out. Catherine Shepherd, distraught after a lovers' spat, suddenly starts thinking like a cross between Sherlock Holmes and René Descartes? 'Let's see,' she reasons coolly, 'I heard the door slam but I didn't hear Preston drive off. Therefore he must be sitting in the garage, contemplating suicide.' I don't think so. I know we didn't give you much time, but is that the best you could do?"

"What can I say?" C-Sharp protested. "That's the way it happened."

"No," Phillips said. "The way it happened was that Preston came downstairs and talked to you. He told you to wait for three to five minutes after he slammed the door, and then to rush upstairs and feed the suicide theory to Catherine. I want you to tell me if that's the way it happened, C-Sharp. And I'm liable to get cross if you lie to me again."

"Have it your way," C-Sharp said, shrugging.

"One more chance," Phillips said.

C-Sharp put his hands on his hips, bent slightly at the waist, and carefully examined the floorboards for five seconds.

"This stays here, right?" he demanded.

"As in no one tells Cindy?" Phillips responded. "Let me

put it this way. Cindy's going to get told in the next five minutes unless you cut to the chase."

"Okay," C-Sharp said then, his voice flat and dull. "That was the plan. What you said. And that's the way it went down."

"Very well," Phillips said. "Now, C-Sharp, if I were you, I'd look for ways to keep Avery Phillips happy from this moment until I lose interest in this tawdry little farce."

He pivoted sharply away from C-Sharp and began marching toward the stairs. Turning to follow him, Michaelson was mildly surprised to see a striking, dark-haired woman in a close-fitting, ankle-length dress of pink satin starting up the stairs. His first, improbable thought was, Liza Minelli—here? Then something about her eyes tickled a key in the back of Michaelson's memory. When he got a full look at her face as she passed through a puddle of light, his double take achieved full wattage. A moment or two later, he heard Phillips, already halfway down the stairs and passing the pink-clad figure.

"Evening, Janos," he said.

"*Gays and Dolls*," Willie sighed with contentment. "*Luke Be a Lady Tonight.*"

Michaelson had managed to wipe any suggestion of surprise off his features by the time he was out on the sidewalk with Phillips and his two companions, trudging toward the spot where Phillips had illegally parked his Mercedes sport utility vehicle.

"Can I cadge a ride back to my apartment?" Michaelson asked. "Save me interzone cab fare."

"Sure," Phillips said.

Michaelson slipped into the backseat with Phillips, blandly ignoring the intense scrutiny that Project directed at them from the passenger seat in front. Willie drove.

"I take it you're not going to tell me what Demarest went after for you," Michaelson said.

"No, I'm not. Why should I?"

"To show that you learn from experience. A clearheaded gent like you should think, 'I mustn't leave Michaelson in the dark. That's the mistake I made last time.' You sent Demarest back in blind, and that didn't work out very well, did it?"

"Not 'back in.' I wasn't the one who sent him in the first time."

"We both know who sent him in the first time," Michaelson said. "You were one of the people he showed the receipt and the memo to, and he couldn't figure out why you didn't pat him on the head and tell him what a clever boy he was."

"Poor Preston," Phillips sighed. "He was such a dunderhead."

"But you knew, somehow, that there was in fact something worthwhile still there. Demarest had found it but didn't know what it was. You knew what it was, but you couldn't find it. You decided to have Demarest get it for you, but without telling him what he was looking for. The end result was that the information stayed in and a corpse came out."

"He knew the risks," Phillips said.

"I keep hearing that. Now you know the risks."

"Risks run both ways."

"Before, perhaps," Michaelson conceded. "You felt you couldn't completely trust Demarest. He was stupid and he thought he was smart, so there were two solid arguments in support of your position. But you can trust me and you know it. If I give you my word, I'll keep it."

"Your word about what?"

"That I'll offer you the same thing the other side is offering me: a seat at the table. If we collaborate and I come up with whatever you're after, we'll shop it jointly or not at all."

"And otherwise?" Phillips asked.

"Every man for himself."

"I'll take my chances."

"I don't understand your position," Michaelson said. "Your approach has cost one human life so far. How much money has to be involved to distort your judgment that badly?"

Phillips scooted around on the satiny black leather to look directly at Michaelson.

"Money is just a way of keeping score," he said. "Triple net, this deal may well end up as a loss. Losses are sometimes useful in my business, of course, and best case maybe there's even a five-figure profit. Nothing like enough to justify the huge financial risk of carrying the house, assuming I can find a way to buy it in the first place."

"Then why?" Michaelson asked.

"They *owe* me," Phillips said with uncharacteristic vehemence. "You're a grunt at Fort Dix, you get to shop at the Post Exchange. You're an officer who spends three years in Germany, you get to bring a BMW with you when you're rotated home. You do what I did, you get to take your opportunities where you find them—and if you find the right one, you get to play at the big table again. They owe *me*; they don't owe you."

"You should be ashamed of yourself," Michaelson said joshingly. "You're letting sentiment interfere with logic."

The huge vehicle pulled up outside Michaelson's Georgetown apartment building. Phillips smiled as he reached across Michaelson and opened the door on his side.

"You've got balls, Richard," he said. "But you don't have any cards. Good night."

Eighteen

Feeling that he'd had about enough sophistication for the night, Michaelson fixed himself a peanut-butter-and-jelly sandwich while he listened to a replay of that afternoon's euro conference blaring on C-SPAN from his living room.

"So which is it?" a television voice demanded as Michaelson spread Jif creamy on white Wonder Bread. "Is the success of the euro inevitable or impossible?"

"It is impossible," the television Michaelson said with unruffled dispassion while the real-life version slathered Welch's grape jam over the peanut butter, "unless 'euro' turns out to be another word for deutschemark. Then it is inevitable."

Michaelson finished making the sandwich, sliced it into triangles, and set it on a china plate. The euro conference wound down rapidly.

"Coming up next," a C-SPAN voice-over interjected then over the mild hubbub of the conference breaking up. "Doctor and Congressman Marcus Humphreys in his

National Press Club address earlier this afternoon."

Michaelson, who had been reaching toward his kitchen radio, stopped as he found his interest unexpectedly piqued by the program note. The idea of watching C-SPAN when he wasn't on it wouldn't ordinarily have occurred to him. He didn't know for sure why the prospect of a canned speech by Marcus Humphreys intrigued him, but he decided impulsively to stick with it instead of turning his radio on to WETA. After all, he told himself with a mental shrug, politics or opera—white noise was white noise.

Carrying his plate and a glass of skim milk into the living room, he nudged a heavy, wooden chessboard aside to make room for the plate on his coffee table. Last month's *Foreign Affairs* struck him as an inspired idea for a coaster. He looked at an empty rostrum on his television screen, waited along with C-SPAN for Marcus Humphreys's appearance, and nibbled at his sandwich while he started thinking.

He thought first about not holding any cards. Why didn't Phillips think Michaelson had any cards? True enough, he'd had to do some bluffing along the way on this one, but up to now Phillips hadn't had the nerve to call him on them. Now, thanks to Connaught, Phillips was no longer the only game in town for Michaelson. Not only that, he'd come up with solid reasons to believe that the item in play here, whatever it might be, was important for partisan and electoral reasons rather than because of national security concerns. So why was Phillips picking now to get all hard-nosed? As long as Phillips hadn't found whatever he was after, how could he ignore anyone who might be able to help him?

Next he thought about dunderheads. About Demarest. About a man coldly exploiting a fragile young woman's suicide-guilt trauma. Or was it coldly? Marjorie had raised

148

an interesting question. Had Demarest acted entirely out of tactical calculation? Or somewhere inside had he enjoyed what he did for its own sake—gotten a perverted thrill out of giving Catherine a psychological flogging from time to time, savoring her desperately panicked reactions to his effortless manipulation?

Humphreys now approached the podium as applause smattered. In an uncommon shot for TV, the camera caught him in full stride during three or four seconds of his approach, showed him nodding and smiling at people standing near the rostrum as he walked past them. He was shorter than Michaelson had expected him to be. But of course, Michaelson reminded himself, like most Americans he had never seen Humphreys except on television. He had unconsciously been expecting a James Earl Jones with Marcus Humphreys's face to approach the podium. On Humphreys's features, as he squared his notes and adjusted the microphone, Michaelson read bedside manner instead of standard-issue eagerness to please.

"Three minutes tops before he quotes Tocqueville," Michaelson murmured around bites of peanut butter and jelly.

He had been keeping his right hand carefully free of the sandwich so that he could use it to grab other things without getting them sticky. He did that now, rummaging through the briefcase he'd tossed at the end of his couch until he came up with Wilcox's Calvert Manor floor plan and with his copy of the police report. Scattering pawns and bishops, he laid the floor plan on the chessboard and examined it while Humphreys's rolling cadences flowed from the television.

"Almost eighty years ago," Humphreys was saying 163 seconds into his speech, "the English writer G. K. Chesterton realized something very singular about the United States while he was touring this country."

149

"Not Tocqueville," Michaelson commented in mild surprise as Humphreys continued.

"Chesterton noticed that, unlike any other country that has ever existed, American nationhood isn't based on race, or blood, or soil, or religion. We are the first country in history whose nationhood is based on an idea. That idea is political equality. To be an American is not to have a particular ancestry or to speak a particular language or to worship God in a particular way. It is to embrace that idea. To be engaged with it. To live it actively. To take part, day in and day out, in the continuing dialogue about that idea that is the essence of the American experience. No secular idea in human history is more breathtaking, more radical, more important. Or, potentially, more dangerous."

Hmm, Michaelson thought, abruptly shaking himself to check cynical reflexes that seemed to be operating with unusual efficiency tonight. No journeyman speechwriter would have penned Humphreys's last sentence. No staff aide who'd been in Washington for more than six weeks would have cleared it. Michaelson began to consider the novel and refreshing possibility that he'd just heard a politician express an original thought.

Cynicism in Washington is like secondhand smoke. With casual and malignant impartiality it infiltrates those who indulge and those who abstain alike. You make it a firm principle never to touch the stuff, and you still come home at night with your eyes red and your throat scratchy and your clothes reeking from it. You could get rid of secondhand smoke, of course, with a shower or a trip to the dry cleaners. Ambient cynicism was harder. You had to think. Once you had enough experience to be any good in Washington, the most baffling locked room you were likely to encounter was your own mind.

Examining the floor plan while he continued to listen to Humphreys's speech, Michaelson began to think that he might just possibly be right about how the murderer had managed Preston Demarest's killing. His first inkling had come when he reviewed the police report inventory of items the crime scene team had found. Now the whole thing—entrance, exit, and murder in between—was coming into interesting focus.

Except, of course, for the nagging detail of who the murderer actually was. He'd had a very satisfactory little theory on that score until an hour or so ago, when he'd realized that C-Sharp couldn't possibly be the killer. No one with the pathological fear of heights that C-Sharp had displayed at the mezzanine railing could have committed this murder. Michaelson was sufficiently eccentric by Washington standards to regard impossibility as a material flaw in a theory about real-world events.

So he had to start over on *who?*

He drank some milk. Could he and Phillips both have been flat-out wrong in rejecting CIA complicity in the murder? Politicized at the top, divided in the middle, demoralized at the bottom—all true, but even so. Onshore homicide, huge risk, scant upside.

And yet, he had to admit, during the Clinton administration (if not before) the CIA had unarguably reached the sorry state of having its director take orders from an unelected hack working for a political party. Once any outfit in the national security business was that far gone, maybe all bets were off. Still, he found it hard to believe. It's one thing for bureaucratic behavior to be irrational. It's something else entirely for it to violate the laws of political physics.

Well, this wasn't getting him anywhere on *who*. He decided provisionally to focus on a different initial question: *What?* What was Phillips after? What had he wanted Demarest to retrieve from Calvert Manor? What was it that made *mobiliers antiques* important, and whatever it was, why did Phillips have to buy the entire house to be sure of getting his hands on it?

"During one of the most desperate hours of our Revolution, just before the surprise attack on Trenton," Humphreys was saying as Michaelson again gave the television his attention, "General Washington issued a famous order: 'The times are perilous and our enterprise of utmost risk. Put none but Americans on guard tonight.'

"I don't know if Thaddeus Praisegod Humphreys, my great-grandfather's great-grandfather, was one of the Continental soldiers who went on guard that night. But he could have been. He was a free man of color, as the polite phrase of the era had it, at the time of the American Revolution. We know he was a man of some property, because when he went to join Washington's army, he provided his own musket, ball, powder, and kit. We can safely assume that he bellyached about his taxes when he quaffed ale with his neighbors after hauling the tobacco he'd grown with his black hands to market. But nobody crosses an icy river on Christmas Eve under the guns of a large fort for lower taxes. Thaddeus Praisegod Humphreys, just like the men on either side of him, put his life on the line for an idea—for what became the American idea."

Michaelson sat quite straight on the couch, eyes riveted for the moment to the television, only a slight quiver in his lips betraying the tingle of excitement racing along his nerves. He was hearing the unstated but unmistakable rationale for Marcus Humphreys's presidential candidacy. The skillfully interwoven, richly textured tapestry of history, race, principle, and circumstance that defined Humphreys's unique moral authority. Humphreys could say with authenticity what would sound platitudinous in the mouth of a white aspirant; and he could say with compelling force what would sound like special interest bleating from a black candidate for whom the American

Revolution was an irrelevant argument between privileged white men about how to divide the spoils of slave labor.

None of which was why Michaelson suddenly bolted from the apartment, leaving half a sandwich on his coffee table and barely taking time to grab his coat. In his mind he saw again a near-perfect mental image of the print Demarest had made and Halliburton had given him: the hotel receipt photographed against the background of old-fashioned script on a different document. He was hurrying through his door now because he had just figured out how Preston Demarest could have had something valuable without knowing it, how Avery Phillips could have known it was valuable without being able readily to retrieve it, why Phillips had insisted on movable items more than one hundred years old being included in the sale of Calvert Manor. He had just figured out what Preston Demarest had lost his life trying to find at Calvert Manor.

Twenty-five minutes later Michaelson was sitting at a table in Cavalier Books's tiny refreshment area, sipping black coffee and neglecting Marjorie Randolph. Having sketched his theory to her, he had now been concentrating for close to a minute on the document Jim Halliburton had entrusted to him years before, which he had picked up at his office on the way over.

"I have a terrible feeling," he murmured, "that I'm right."

"A bracing prospect for us all," Marjorie said.

He glanced up at her, offering a brief smile.

"Would you do me a great favor?" he asked.

"Let you use my telephone?" she guessed. "That's a minor imposition, not a great favor."

"I'm afraid it's not a call I can make with any credibility," he said. "I need you to call the trustee, Ms. Wilcox."

"She certainly won't be in her office at this hour."

"Quite right. Leave a voice mail message that she'll hear first thing in the morning."

"To what effect?" Marjorie asked.

"That you wish to buy the Calvert Manor estate books. Ten thousand dollars or something."

"Based on some fifteen years' experience in the booksellers' trade," Marjorie said, "the Calvert Manor estate books strike me as inventory that is likely to move very slowly. So ten thousand would be roughly nine thousand six hundred more than I'd feel comfortable paying."

"Oh, there's no danger of her accepting the offer," Michaelson said with the insouciant flippancy of someone who wouldn't be writing the check. "She won't make a deal on any estate property without getting everyone involved to sign off on it first."

"Then what's the point?"

"To make her test the market, thereby bluffing Avery Phillips into thinking that I have more cards than he thinks I do."

Marjorie rose and, before strolling toward the stockroom with its desk and telephone, offered Michaelson an expression that mingled tolerance and exasperation. She returned in less than three minutes to confirm that she had completed the mission assigned to her.

"And if I find myself shelling out ten thousand dollars for twenty-odd volumes of bills of exchange for tobacco hogsheads," she warned, "you are going to spend the next five Christmas seasons putting in twelve unpaid hours a day at my cash register."

"Agreed."

"Presumably we'll have nothing further from Wilcox and therefore from Phillips until tomorrow morning," Marjorie said. "Is there anything else on tonight's agenda?"

"Only a trip to the Flogged Cat," Michaelson said.

154

"Flogged Cat?" Marjorie asked, looking puzzled for a moment. "Oh. Club Chat Fouetté. Your translation threw me."

"Isn't it accurate?"

"Literally, yes. But I think the English meaning actually intended is a bit more vulgar."

Michaelson now looked blank for a moment. "Flogged cat. Whipped—my word, I believe you're right."

"You've been to that place once today already. What's there now?"

"A man named Janos who smokes cigars and who makes a very striking woman when he climbs into drag. When I put those two things together, some of the gestures he makes when he indulges in his currently fashionable habit remind me of someone."

"I'll give Carrie the store keys and get my car," Marjorie said.

"No need to sacrifice commercial considerations to our search for the truth," Michaelson said. "I don't think there's much point in getting there before ten-thirty."

"What's magic about ten-thirty?"

"That should be a few minutes before C-Sharp's second set starts."

"You want to talk to him again?" Marjorie asked.

"No. I want to talk to Cindy."

Nineteen

A blast of sound hit Michaelson and Marjorie with literally physical force as they stepped into Club Chat Fouetté at ten twenty-seven. Eighty seconds later, when they had adapted sufficiently to the decibel level to be able to pick out individual words here and there, they would realize they were hearing the finale chorus of "Pretty Girls Smoking Cigarettes."

Michaelson sensed that the room was fairly crowded, but he could see almost nothing in the smoky blackness that separated them from the stage. He and Marjorie sought the end of the bar while they waited for C-Sharp's set to end and the lights to come up. Michaelson ordered chardonnay for Marjorie and Johnnie Walker Black for himself.

"We're in luck," Marjorie shouted when the order arrived. "Neither drink came with an umbrella."

"I told you this was a high-class place," Michaelson answered.

With a final, screaming D chord and a strobe effect that

could not have been called tastefully understated, the song ended. Whoever was handling the light board teased the crowd a bit with spots and floods, milking the applause, cheers, and whistles that greeted the performance. Then with the other lights cut, the main spot picked out a dark-haired figure coming toward the stage in a sparkling white dress, off the shoulder and ankle length, left side slit from hip to heel to display a long leg that stood up very well to the exposure.

"Janos," Michaelson whispered to Marjorie.

"Right."

Janos reached center stage and appropriated C-Sharp's microphone as the whistling got louder and what sounded like good-natured catcalls mingled with the cheers. He turned flirtatious eyes toward the crowd.

"Get a grip on it, you animals," he growled into the microphone with a smirk. Laughter greeted the crack. "Don't make me come down there and discipline you."

Laughter, much louder this time, mixed with cheers and enthusiastic applause. Janos turned slyly toward C-Sharp, wagging an admonitory finger.

"You shouldn't encourage girls to smoke cigarettes," he scolded as rolling laughter engulfed the room. "The First Lady says they're very bad for us."

From the back of the stage one of the band members stepped toward the spotlight, wearing a Hillary Clinton mask. C-Sharp leaned into the microphone.

"Hillary says have a cigar," he said.

"Good idea," Janos said, accepting what to Michaelson's nonexpert eyes looked like a Macunado from the masked band member.

He leaned forward to accept a light offered by C-Sharp, doing an apparently quite conscious imitation of Lauren Bacall in *To Have and Have Not*. Enthusiastic cheers greeted the first puff of smoke that he blew toward the ceiling.

157

"All right," Janos said then, turning back toward the crowd. "C-Sharp and his little friends are going to take a break. Next set in forty-five minutes. Meanwhile, this is *not* open-mike night, so unless you have a contract, stay off the stage."

Enough lights now came on to leave the room in only semidarkness. Michaelson could see that it was about ninety percent full, with four-fifths of the patrons male. He wondered if the club had done this well on weeknights before Demarest's murder lent the place a morbidly fascinating association with violent death.

He spotted Cindy at an out-of-the-way table, just beyond the bar and to one side of the stage. She was alone at the moment, but he assumed that C-Sharp would be joining her as soon as he had toweled off and done a quick postmortem with his band. With Marjorie in his wake, Michaelson hustled toward the young woman.

"You're in an abstemious minority," Michaelson said as they reached her. "Ninety-eight percent of the people in here seem to be smoking."

"I pick my spots," Cindy said without looking up at him.

"May we join you briefly?"

"No."

"Thank you."

Michaelson pulled out one of the chairs for Marjorie, then seated himself between the two women. Cindy glared at him.

"I said no," she told him sharply.

"Clumsy of me, I know," Michaelson said. "But we don't really have time for finesse. It is quite important that, without further delay, you give me the page you took from the Calvert Manor estate books."

This drew a shrug and a "Now what?" sigh from Cindy.

"What are you talking about?" she demanded. "Not that I particularly give a shit."

"I'm talking about something that could endanger what's left of your sister's sanity and possibly her life," Michaelson said.

Cindy's head whipped around and her eyes flashed. Michaelson got a particularly good look at the eyes because Cindy grabbed a fistful of his shirt and pulled him several inches closer to her.

"That's not funny, goddammit," she snapped.

Michaelson made no effort to escape from her grip. When he spoke his voice was matter-of-fact, as if he were a young desk officer summarizing overnight cable traffic for a bored area director at the State Department.

"On February the third of this year," he said, "you were awakened by a fight between your sister and Preston Demarest. I'm not sure what point the battle had reached when you got there. It doesn't matter. Somewhere along the line, either before or after C-Sharp hustled upstairs with alarmist speculations about Demarest's intentions and your sister hysterically took the bait, you saw something that told you what the fight was about."

Cindy let go of Michaelson's shirt and sank all the way back into her own chair.

"You have me confused with Kinsey Milhone in *B Is for Brainy*," she said. "I'm not that smart."

Michaelson smoothed his shirtfront, unknotted his bow tie, and with unruffled calm began retying it.

"Nonsense," he said affably. "The venue for the fight was the library, where at least one light was on even though it was the small hours of the morning. One volume of the estate books was pulled onto the worktable and opened in the lamplight to a particular page. You are in fact quite bright, but you didn't have to be a genius to conclude that the fight had something to do with Demarest's surreptitious interest in that book."

"Oh sure," Cindy said, looking pointedly away.

"Not so much to put together, really," Michaelson said. "With Catherine contentedly sleeping, Demarest sneaks into the library and pokes his nose into a two-hundred-year-old bound volume of estate records. Being less than accomplished at this line of work, he doesn't notice that Catherine has awakened and gone in search of him until she's in the doorway, observing him in his compromising labors. She asks him what's going on. Demarest is less than inspired when it comes to improvisation, so his answer is unsatisfactory. He resorts to bluster, angry reaction feeds on angry reaction, and in the midst of the altercation you come on the scene to figure things out. You knew that the page was important, although you may not have known why, so you took it out of the book and put it someplace where Demarest couldn't find it."

Cindy turned back to him.

"You're making this up, aren't you?" she said.

"Not altogether. You see, there's a core fact that needs to be explained. Demarest had weeks of opportunity after February third to find that page again, but he couldn't do it. While Demarest admittedly wasn't the brightest roman candle in the fireworks display, he should certainly have been able to find the thing again if it hadn't been removed. Avery Phillips, moreover, knew that what he wanted Demarest to retrieve had been in the estate books at one time, which is why he conditioned his purchase offer on including them with the house under the obscure label *mobiliers antiques*. But he feared it wasn't there anymore, which is why he had to buy the whole house. Conclusion: Demarest was after a particular page from the estate books, and he couldn't find it because you had taken it."

Cindy held up her index and little fingers in a school yard horns symbol.

"Bull*shit*," she said.

"Skip it," Michaelson said. "I'm not trying to get you to admit anything. I know I'm right, and I know you know I'm right. What you also need rather urgently to understand is that Avery Phillips is *not* a dimwit. He wants the document, he's coming after it, and when he does he'll pick on Catherine."

"Like there's something you could do about *that*," Cindy said as anger and alarm flashed across her face.

"There is, actually," Michaelson said. "Avery and I have been dealing with each other for many years. He lives by his own rules, but he's a professional. He doesn't believe in wasted motion. Once he knows I have the thing, he'll stop bothering other people for it."

"Why wouldn't I just give it to him, then, if I had it?" Cindy asked, a gamine-ish little moue marring her features.

"Because if you did that, I wouldn't have any reason to keep quiet about why Preston Demarest was killed," Michaelson said in a silky voice that Marjorie always found a bit chilling. "Or about how he was killed. Or about who killed him."

An uncomfortable silence followed, broken after about five seconds by a familiar voice.

"Hey, people, what's happening?" C-Sharp asked.

Twenty

No one who had seen C-Sharp cowering on the mezzanine late that afternoon, Michaelson thought, could have imagined the confident, smiling, almost charismatic figure who stood before them now. Testosterone all but splashing out of his ears, he was glowing from the rush of the successful performance, radiant with the memory of the cheers, exuding not just the thrill of acclaim but the awe of experiencing it at this level for the first time. Michaelson wondered, with a touch of poignance, if what he'd just witnessed would turn out to be the prelude to charted songs and performances before tens of thousands at a time or, instead, the bittersweet highlight of a dream that never quite happened.

"Please join us," Marjorie said to C-Sharp after several moments had passed without Cindy issuing the invitation. "You obviously gave the crowd here what they came for."

C-Sharp sat down at the table, pretending to shrug the compliment off but clearly pleased by it. A waiter hustled over and put what looked like bourbon and Coke in front of C-Sharp. He picked up the tumbler, sniffed it first, and smiled before taking a generous swallow.

"Did I hear you say you figured out who killed P.D.?" he asked after the drink. "I thought the heat were chalking that one up to"—here C-Sharp closed his eyes and turned his face toward the ceiling, knitting his brows in an ostentatious display of concentration—"awww-toe ee-rotic misadventure."

"Or suicide," Cindy said.

"Same thing," C-Sharp said. He switched to a surfer-dude smile and waited politely for the applause.

"You may well be right," Michaelson said. "If they were calling it murder, they would presumably have questioned me by now, for example. And they haven't."

"End of mystery, then," C-Sharp said with a boyishly mischievous grin. "Let's talk some more about me."

"The police are only human, after all," Michaelson continued. "It would be a bit awkward to say Demarest was murdered when there's no apparent way for a killer to have gotten into or out of the room where it happened."

"Now see," C-Sharp said, "that's the limitations of reality for you. On *The X-Files* that would simply be no problem at all."

"It's not actually all that much of a problem in the real world, either," Michaelson said offhandedly. "But then there are some things the police don't know yet. The shoes, for example."

"C-Sharp," Cindy interjected with a kind of languid abruptness, "would you do something really special for me?"

"Right here in front of all these people?" C-Sharp asked as his eyebrows reached heroically for his scalp.

"Oh, that's *very* naughty," Cindy scolded playfully, tapping C-Sharp's nose with the tip of her finger and favoring him with a point-blank volley of what Michaelson took to be her undiluted charm. "But I want something else. First."

"Name it."

"A Cohiba Panatela. You'll go over to the bar and get one for me? Please?"

"No shit?" C-Sharp asked, surprise and distaste competing for control of his expression. "I know stogies were chick-chic for about fifteen minutes two years ago, but that's sorta been-there-done-that for you, isn't it?"

Cindy waited two beats, offering a look that Steichen might have photographed and titled *Actors Studio Exercise no. 38: Ingenue Pouting*. Then she spoke.

"Not comp, 'cause then they'll try to palm off a Monte Cristo on you. Just have them put it on my tab for tonight."

"Cohiba Panatela," C-Sharp muttered, giving the table an I'm-*really*-being-a-good-sport-about-this slap as he rose. "*Not* Monte Cristo. Got it."

Cindy turned back toward Michaelson as soon as C-Sharp was out of earshot.

"All right," she snapped decisively. "The shoes. You've got *maybe* five minutes. Let's hear it."

"When Marjorie and I drove up to Calvert Manor the day of the murder, Demarest was shoveling snow off the porch roof. Yet when he came downstairs a few minutes later there wasn't a hint of damp on his shoes. He walked across a parquet floor without leaving so much as a water spot. How did he manage that, do you suppose?"

"He was the kind of guy who ironed his underpants," Cindy said. "Figure it out."

"I have. He changed shoes before he came down. He apparently had an extra pair there because he was—"

"—shacked up half the time with Cathy, right," Cindy said with exasperated impatience. "Okay, he changed shoes. So what?"

"So the police didn't find an extra pair of his shoes upstairs," Michaelson said. "They found the pair that he must

164

have changed out of in a gym bag in his car. Where the murderer put them in the confusion while everyone was running out of the house."

"*Time*-out," Cindy said, making a palm-on-fingertips signal with her hands. "Rewind. Take two. *What* are you talking about?"

"The murderer got to the room where Demarest was killed by going along the porch roof," Michaelson said. "Wearing Demarest's shoes. That's why all the footprints the police found on the roof matched his shoes. If the footprints had been made in snow or mud, the police might have been able to tell that some of the prints were left by someone else, lighter and with a smaller foot. But all they had were partial damp outlines, so there was nothing to distinguish the traces left by Demarest himself during his snow shoveling from those the murderer left."

"Hellll-ooohhh," Cindy said in a scornful singsong. "Planet Earth to old fart. You can't get *into* the room where Armani-boy was killed from the roof."

"True," Michaelson said as he pulled out the floor plan and unfolded it on the table. "But you *can* get into the adjoining bathroom from there. And the bathroom leads to the murder room."

"Except that the bathroom door was closed and locked from Preston's side," Cindy said.

"Right," Michaelson said. "*After* he was killed."

"Why *after*?" Cindy demanded. "Let alone *how*, which looks like another biggie. Seems to me he would have locked it himself, to make sure no one intruded on him while he was beating his meat."

"I think the sexual activity he had in mind was emphatically nonsolitary," Michaelson said. "Given what he planned to do, I think on the contrary that he ensured intrusion by the person he planned to do it with. Which is why he let the murderer in."

"My eyes just officially glazed over," Cindy said.

"Someone accusing me of murder?" C-Sharp asked cheerfully as he returned. "Here's your stick, sunshine. I even had the bartender clip it for you."

Michaelson turned his attention to C-Sharp while Cindy yanked an ashtray and matchbook from the center of the table and set about lighting the cigar.

"Until this afternoon I was actually quite sure you were the killer," Michaelson said. "I assumed your friends downstairs either weren't paying attention or were covering for you, and that you'd managed to slip outside and somehow get to the roof without leaving any trail."

"Not guilty," C-Sharp said with the now-familiar palms-out gesture as he sat down.

"I know. You couldn't possibly have faked the pathological terror you obviously felt up on the mezzanine a few hours ago. Your morbid fear of even modest heights puts you in the clear."

"Hey, don't remind me about this afternoon unless you want a meal, six drinks, and two peyote buttons all over your suit," C-Sharp said. "But I'll take being off the hook, even if it's only your hook."

"You're welcome," Michaelson said evenly, glancing out of the corner of his eye at Cindy. "And we might as well clear half the human race while we're at it. No one went upstairs during the conference call, and no one climbed onto the roof from outside. An expert might have been able to manage it without leaving a trace anywhere at ground level, but no one at Calvert Manor that afternoon was in the expert category. The murderer had to be on the second floor of Calvert Manor when the conference call started. So we can start calling the murderer 'she.' "

"No kiddin'," C-Sharp said. "Blows me away, man. But you know what? Everyone on the second floor except P.D. himself was *on the phone* during the call. On. The. Phone.

The which there ain't any of in the room where P. D. bought it. Phones, that is."

"Two," Cindy said, making a basketball ref's count-it signal with her left hand. "And everyone on the phone is on record as saying something at least every five minutes."

"What I'm sayin'," C-Sharp said. "So what's your pitch? That one of the ladies traipsed around on the roof, got into P.D.'s room, aced him, started a fire, got out again, somehow locked the doors behind her, got back to where she was in the first place, and got back on the phone? All in five minutes? Tell ya somethin', bro: never happened."

"The *phones*, of *course*," Michaelson said, smacking his forehead with the heel of his hand. "You're absolutely right. Why, I never even thought of that. You've saved me from a very embarrassing blunder."

"Hey, no charge, man." C-Sharp drained his bourbon and Coke and pulled himself from his chair. "Well, got to hit the little boys room and talk to the guys before last set. See ya."

He ambled off, swimming through a sea of admiration on his way. The three people still at the table watched him until he had disappeared around the far end of the stage.

"Hm," Michaelson said then, looking again at the floor plan. "Shall we see if there's some way around C-Sharp's searing insight about the phones?"

"Not interested," Cindy said.

"Do you think C-Sharp might be interested? Or the police? Or Avery Phillips?"

"I thought Avery Phillips was interested in documents, not floor plans," Cindy asked impatiently as she waved rich blue smoke away from her face with her left hand and settled back with the cigar poised pertly between the first two fingers of her right. "Which do you want to talk about?"

"The document, if I have to choose," Michaelson said.

"I wanted it when I walked in here. I still want it."

"How much do you want it? And I mean that just the way it sounded."

"If you give me the estate book page I described," Michaelson said, "I'll make sure Phillips knows I have it and that he stops looking for it at Calvert Manor."

"And?" Cindy prompted.

"And I will not tell the police, or Phillips, or anyone else, that Catherine Shepherd killed Preston Demarest."

Sighing with relief and sagging back in her chair as if a year's buildup of tension had just flowed out of her body, Cindy consigned her cigar to the ashtray. Then she reached into a small backpack that was apparently serving as her purse tonight and pulled out the large Bible Marjorie had seen on her second trip to Calvert Manor. She opened the cover and began delicately removing the protective glassine flyleaf. If she flips to a weirdly apropos passage in Proverbs or Judges, Marjorie thought, I'm definitely stepping up my church attendance.

Cindy didn't. When she had the glassine off, she began, as Michaelson and Marjorie looked on in breath-held fascination, to unwrap the stiff, yellowed paper that had been slipped over the Bible's cover as an impromptu, homemade dust jacket. Michaelson almost gasped as he suddenly realized that Cindy had treated centuries-old parchment that could crumble to dust from the slightest touch like dime-store construction paper, creasing and folding it to fit the Bible and now, just as causally, exponentially increasing the stress on the brittle document by reversing the process. He winced. He fully expected to see this document utterly demolished before his eyes in the next few seconds. The danger struck him as chillingly symptomatic: history being literally destroyed not by malice, not even by stupidity, but by indifference.

As Cindy pulled the paper away, Michaelson could see

familiar, faded script on the side that had been hidden. Not quite calligraphy by eighteenth-century standards, but a fair hand in any age. He pretended to scratch his nose so that he could hide a quick intake of breath behind his fingers. A palm-sized chunk of parchment chose that moment to come off in Cindy's hand and disintegrate on the table.

"Shit," Cindy said thoughtfully.

"It must have an unusually high linen content or the entire thing would be just so much dust by now," Marjorie said.

Proceeding more carefully and, somehow, doing remarkably little additional damage to the document, Cindy finished removing it from the Bible and laid it on the table, bent in a rictus that was almost painful to look at. She leaned across the table toward Michaelson, close enough that he could smell the cigar smoke on her breath.

"All right," she said. "We have a deal, right?"

"Right," Michaelson answered. "I've given my word and I'll keep it."

"And I should believe that because—"

"Because in the modest position I occupy in Washington at the moment, without office, power, or prospects, my word is all I have. Unless everyone in town knows they can take it to the bank, I'm finished."

Cindy slid the page across the table. With infinite delicacy, pushing it gently at the edges an inch at a time, Michaelson turned it around so that he and Marjorie could both examine the text right side up. He recognized it, for he had seen part of it before in a grainy photograph with a hotel receipt on top of it.

"You're going to have to help me," he said to Marjorie. "In this light, my eyes aren't up to two-hundred-year-old handwriting."

"My privilege," Marjorie said with complete sincerity. She began reading:

This INDENTURE, made, done, sealed, and delivered at Annapolis Courthouse, Anne Arundel County, Maryland, this fourth day of April in the Year of Our Lord One-thousand-seven-hundred-and-ninety-seven and of the independence of the United States of America the twenty-second—
WITNESSETH:
I, Colonel Charles James Calvert, Esq., the Fourth of that Name, of Calvert Manor, Prince Georges County, Maryland, for and in consideration of receipt in hand of a bill of exchange in the amount of Three-Hundred-and-no-One-Hundredths Dollars ($300), and for other good and valuable consideration, the receipt and sufficiency of which I do herewith acknowledge, do hereby bargain and sell, transfer, and convey, unto Thaddeus Praisegod Humphreys, freeholder of Calvert County, Maryland, in full title and free, to have and to hold, with no liens, encumbrances or other hindrance whatsoever, from this day forward, as his chattel property, the slave TOBY, a Guinea male of twenty-one years more or less and in fair health.

Signed and sealed as of the day and date first above written.
/s/ Col. Charles James Calvert IV Esq.
Locus Sigili

Michaelson and Marjorie both looked up at Cindy, who gazed back with the mildly baffled detachment of the only one in the room who doesn't get the joke. Michaelson was convinced by now that she was thoroughly intelligent—indeed, brilliant. Could she possibly be so innocent of history—not just without historical knowledge, but lacking any sense of the past whatever, any instinct about it—that she didn't see the importance of this fragment? Didn't understand what a bombshell it would be, in a country where race was the subtext of all political discourse, to reproduce this document on the front page of *The Washington Post?*

She didn't, and there seemed no point in trying to explain. And so Michaelson without further comment took sole and very gingerly possession of documentary evidence that a black candidate for President of the United States was the descendant of a black slaveowner.

Twenty-one

Marjorie had seen some odd things in the more than thirty years she had known Michaelson, but the square baking pan filled a quarter-inch deep with table salt sitting next to his sink struck her as off-the-charts. The box of Baggies resting a few feet away was normal enough. But then Michaelson running tap water over very thin fishing line added another bizarre touch.

It was just after nine on Friday morning. She wouldn't be going in to Cavalier Books until around two that afternoon. She would then be there until after midnight, which meant that she should be sleeping now. Instead, she was watching Michaelson prepare what looked like a rather lame junior high school science-fair project.

"Are you comfortable with what we're doing?" she asked.

"No."

"It could destroy Catherine emotionally. I mean push her all the way over the edge. Move her from functional neurotic to drooling basket case."

"There's a grave risk of that," Michaelson agreed. "Now that we have the indenture and can deal with it as we think best, we could wash our hands of the murder, as the police have. If we do that, Catherine's emotional destruction won't be a grave risk anymore. It will become an apodictic certainty."

"Because of Phillips, or Connaught? Or something else?"

"Phillips, mostly. If we handle the indenture exactly right and don't shrink from a little bullying, we can probably neutralize Connaught."

"Have you told Phillips yet that you have the indenture?" Marjorie asked.

"I left a message for him as soon as I had the thing in a safe place."

"Good. The trustee responded very early this morning to my offer for the estate books. She said there's another player in the picture and she wants sealed bids. Your message to Phillips may save him ten thousand dollars or so, as well as reducing his interest in Calvert Manor and those who live there."

"Reducing but not eliminating, unfortunately," Michaelson said. "He now knows that he can't get the indenture through Catherine, but there's still the matter of Demarest passing away."

"Do you think he suspects Catherine?"

"I don't know. But he undoubtedly recognizes Catherine as the weak link. She'll be the first target of his inquiries unless we convince him to stop making them. That means our choice is starkly simple: Go forward, or write Catherine off."

"All of this over a piece of parchment two centuries old," Marjorie mused. "A historical curiosity. It seems surreal for savvy people to imagine it having a genuine impact on a presidential campaign."

Michaelson drew the saturated fishing line through the salt-filled baking pan.

"Logically, of course, you're clearly right," he said. "But we're not talking about logic. We're talking about what makes people feel psychologically threatened, what makes them lash out irrationally and close their minds."

"People are threatened by what they don't know," Marjorie said, nodding.

"And even more threatened by subversion of what they think they do know. They have a nice, straightforward, Cinerama view of the world. Suddenly they find themselves looking at a gritty documentary without any soft-focus shots. The reaction is anger, denial, and hysteria—not logical dispassion."

Michaelson took a round cake pan out of his freezer and broke a tray of ice cubes into it.

"In a political campaign that indenture could be what the French call a 'provocation,' " Marjorie said. "A fact that shouldn't be spoken even if it's true."

"Or especially if it's true."

"What in the world are you doing now?" she asked.

"Making little ones out of big ones."

Michaelson laid the salt-caked fishing line on an ice cube, a few millimeters from its end. He let the salt eat through the cube for a few moments, then pressed and sawed with the string until a thin slice of the cube came free. He popped it into a Baggie and tossed the Baggie into the freezer. Then, patiently, he began to repeat the process.

"Is that as tedious as it looks?" Marjorie asked.

"Entirely."

Two minutes later he had five more Baggies in the freezer.

"We don't really have any choice, do we?" she asked then. "About Catherine, I mean."

"I wish we did."

174

"And I'm the one who has to talk to her, aren't I?"

Michaelson looked at Marjorie with sympathy and respect. She would give anything, he knew, for him to say no, he could handle it. But she knew the truth as well as he did.

"You're the only one who can do it," he said. "You're the only chance she has."

Twenty-two

A Cohiba Panatela doesn't taste bad at all when you smoke it, Cindy reflected as she spat her second brushful of toothpaste into the sink around ten o'clock the following Sunday morning. The problem is that then you keep on tasting it for about a week. She'd had her first a few months ago, last November. C-Sharp had fetched her fifth during the Marjorie/Michaelson chat Wednesday night. She now figured she'd have her next one, maybe—never.

After a throatful of Scope, she returned to her bedroom, where C-Sharp contentedly snored, presumably lost in blissful dreams of cheering crowds. She slipped into slacks of khaki denim and grabbed the first T-shirt in her dresser drawer. It was pale blue, featuring a male and a female head in white caricature with a bit of once-topical dialogue overlaid in black: "That's hard to swallow, Mr. President."/"You just said a mouthful, Monica."

Cindy's first misgiving came when she reached the top of the stairs and caught the smell of bacon frying. This didn't compute. Eyes narrowing in puzzled alarm, she hustled downstairs to find Catherine in a sunshine-yellow dress covered by a hunter-green apron. At least she skipped the pearls and high heels, Cindy thought. Catherine was tending a griddle full of bacon, while more than a dozen cooked strips drained on a paper towel–covered plate.

" 'Morning, Cindy," Catherine said brightly with a glance over her shoulder. "Be a lamb and put that bacon on a clean plate, then take it out to the buffet in the dining room with the other food, would you?"

Wary eyes fixed on her sister, Cindy dumped the bacon onto a white china plate and sidled into the dining room with it—where she very nearly dropped it, along with her jaw. Describing the spread that covered the buffet with an offhand reference to "other food" struck Cindy as roughly equivalent to calling World War II a "scrap." Three flavors of bagels, white, light wheat, and whole-wheat toast, all spread deftly with margarine; mounds of fresh fruit; four carafes of fruit juice; pots of coffee and tea; and scrambled eggs bubbling invitingly in a warming pan. In a house that at the moment sheltered a total of three people, Catherine had covered the buffet with enough food for a marine platoon.

Cindy debated with herself for a moment about how best to react. Pretend that she didn't notice anything out of the ordinary? Approach it with calm determination, the way the experts say you should when your seven-year-old starts swearing? Or, she thought with a mental shrug, why not just be myself: direct and tactless?

"What's the Stepford Wife number all about?" she called from the dining room. "I had this vague idea you were going to church or something. I mean, wouldn't this be like a five-day supply of bacon even if C-Sharp and I ate bacon, which I don't and C-Sharp shouldn't?"

"We're having guests for brunch," Catherine yelled back. "Your call, but you might want to put on something a tiny bit dressier."

Cindy strode back into the kitchen but stopped abruptly in the doorway. Her eyes widened and her tongue undertook an urgent search for saliva to swallow. Catherine was holding a long, black-handled, thick-bladed carving knife. And smiling just a bit oddly.

Offering Cindy a genial nod, Catherine used the tip of the knife to separate three more strips of raw bacon from the second package of the stuff she had opened. Cindy expelled a long breath.

"What guests?" Cindy managed to ask.

The doorbell rang.

"That's some of them now, unless I miss my bet," Catherine said. "Would you—"

"I'll get it," Cindy said quickly. "Just please don't ask me to be a lamb again."

As she strode to the front door, Cindy felt the knot of anxiety in her gut swelling into something uncomfortably close to panic. For a wild moment she considered offering a head fake to whoever turned out to be at the door and then running off through the snow to someplace reasonably sane. She fought the impulse back. She opened the door. And she gasped.

"Good morning, Miss Shepherd," Avery Phillips said. "I think the other Miss Shepherd is expecting us. May we come in?"

Cindy stepped back to admit Phillips, quickly followed by Willie and a two-wheel handcart pushed by Project. On the handcart was a trunk that Cindy thought must have been left over from the stateroom scene in *A Night at the Opera*.

"Michaelson has talked to you, right?" she asked.

"Yes, and did his best not to seem to be gloating. Outsmarted me, which I don't mind, and then outfoxed me, which I do. So to get what I want I'll have to deal with him instead of the Shepherd squirearchy."

"What's in the trunk?"

"If there's an outlet somewhere in the house that'll accept a three-prong plug, it's an advanced audiovisual telecommunications center. Otherwise, it's a very expensive doorstop."

"What's it for?" Cindy asked.

The doorbell rang.

"That'd be Michaelson," Phillips said. "Why don't you ask him about the trunk? I'm just following orders."

Cindy opened the front door, where Michaelson and Marjorie waited patiently. Cindy would ordinarily have gaped at the Stanley stainless steel Thermos Michaelson was holding, but her reactive capacities were running on empty at the moment. Catherine glided into the entrance hall, apron doffed.

"Welcome, everybody," she called gaily. "You're just in time for brunch. The buffet is in the dining room. I'm afraid we're a bit informal. I hope you don't mind serving yourselves."

"Yeah," Cindy said dryly. "We haven't been able to get good help since the War. The Boer War."

"May I put this in the freezer?" Michaelson asked, tendering the Thermos with two hands as if it were a prize vintage pinot noir.

"Let me take it for you," Catherine said.

"Do you mind if Willie sets our video toys up in the living room?" Phillips asked.

"*After* we eat," Catherine said firmly over her shoulder.

"Can someone just explain what's going on?" Cindy asked.

"*While* we eat," Catherine said.

Cindy still held back, her expression dubious. C-Sharp

picked that moment to appear in the dining-room doorway, a strip of bacon in one hand and the remains of another disappearing into his mouth.

"Bacon's awesome," he opined.

This assessment resolved the issue. In less than five minutes the eight people were seated at the dining-room table before plates filled—and in Project's case, heaped—with food. A bit forced at first, the conviviality became steadily more real under the stimulus of caffeine, vitamin C, and cholesterol, helped along by Phillips's diverting explanations of the various ways impressive amounts of money could be legally earned without incurring any obligation to pay federal income tax.

It was C-Sharp who introduced the topic that, like a well-crafted simile, explained the meeting without calling attention to itself. Glancing around appraisingly after Phillips finished hymning the delights of accelerated depreciation, he swallowed the last of a toast-and-scrambled-egg sandwich and grinned slyly.

"This is really about P.D., right?" he asked. "I mean, heat's lost interest because they think it's accidental, but some of us aren't buying that, so we're going to rehash it, am I right?"

"The police know perfectly well that Preston Demarest was murdered," Michaelson said. "They've lost interest because it has been hinted to them by people whose good opinion their superiors covet that continuing the investigation can do no good and much harm. And because they've been given some information about Mr. Demarest's background that puts his victimization rather low on the list of constabulary priorities. That's surmise, by the way, but it's clearly the most plausible explanation for what began as a very aggressive and competent investigation suddenly aborting."

"And you're telling us this because—" C-Sharp prompted.

"Because the police aren't the only ones involved, and others with a stake in this matter aren't so easily turned aside. We are here to satisfy those people about how Demarest's murder occurred, and convince them to let things lie where they fell."

Cindy shot Michaelson a look of angry surprise. He ignored it. He let his eyes deliberately survey the faces around the table. Catherine's expression suggested polite interest, as if another guest had asked Michaelson to explain the International Monetary Fund and it was her duty to listen with at least a semblance of attention. Marjorie's eyes were sharp and alert, shifting their gaze rapidly from Phillips to C-Sharp to Cindy. Phillips had his Zen-master mask on, hooded eyes turned steadily in Michaelson's direction. Willie was looking thoughtfully at Catherine. C-Sharp had picked a windowpane in the background between Michaelson and Catherine and focused a look of bemused tolerance on it. Project, busily shoveling fruit from his plate to his mouth, looked covetously at the eggs and bacon still in the warming trays.

"I believe you have the floor," Phillips said to Michaelson.

"We start with Andrew Shepherd," Michaelson said. "He was, among other things, a businessman whose work took him behind what used to be the Iron Curtain. Like many people in that position, he allowed himself to be debriefed by the CIA when he returned from those trips."

"You mean we're gonna pin this on the spooks?" C-Sharp demanded, shaking his head with a disbelieving smile.

"No," Michaelson said. "The Central Intelligence Agency had no reason to kill Preston Demarest, and if it had killed him, he wouldn't have died the way he did. The quality of leadership at that outfit has declined somewhat in recent years, but it isn't yet being run by people who think you can ward off unpleasant publicity by killing an American citizen in the epicenter of American political media. The only people I know of who do think so have jobs as script consultants in Hollywood."

"Then what—" C-Sharp started to ask.

"As my mother used to say," Phillips interjected, "if you keep your eyes and ears open and your mouth shut, you might learn something."

"To continue," Michaelson said. "Andrew Shepherd's wife divorced him at a time when he was going through a psychological crisis, wondering about the worth of his life and career. In this condition, he found himself susceptible to advances by men who claimed to find him attractive or fascinating. That strikes me as very human, although I recognize that there are different views on the matter. I suppose any who are without sin should feel free to cast the first stone."

"I don't see any takers," Marjorie said.

Project, however, glanced up sharply from his freshly filled plate with a look suggesting that he was striving valiantly to assimilate puzzling data.

"Steady, tiger," Phillips said calmly. "In the words of that remarkable woman, Saint Teresa of Avila, 'Humility is truth.' "

"Through an unforeseeable combination of vexatious circumstances, unfortunately," Michaelson continued, "Mr. Shepherd's predilections led to an experience that was quite traumatic for both him and Catherine. The details needn't concern us. Its significance for present purposes is that it resulted in psychological counseling, generating treatment records that should have been kept highly confidential but weren't."

182

"Well, that narrows things down a bit, doesn't it?" Cindy muttered.

"Fast-forward to a little over four years ago," Michaelson said. "Andrew Shepherd learned that he had inoperable stomach cancer. He decided to take his own life. He arranged his affairs and made sure that his family was properly provided for. Then he did one more thing. He felt that Cindy was far less fragile emotionally than Catherine. So he took some pains to ensure that Cindy rather than Catherine would find his body. He thought that Cindy would be able to get the situation under control and spare Catherine the worst of the ordeal. Unfortunately, again, his plans miscarried."

"That's enough," Cindy snapped. "Cathy doesn't have to sit here and take this in her own house."

"Steady, tiger," Catherine said evenly. "In the immortal words of that remarkable woman Lesley Gore, 'It's my party and I'll cry if I want to.' "

"My surmise," Michaelson said, "and that's all it is, is that Andrew Shepherd killed himself less than an hour before he expected Cindy to come home, and several hours before Catherine was due. The Washington area, however, was hit by a snowstorm. The combined incompetence of Washington drivers and its snow-removal crew created the usual, grossly disproportionate gridlock. A trip that should have taken Cindy fifteen minutes consumed over four hours. Catherine, traveling from a different place by a route that didn't take her through Washington, got home before Cindy and found the body."

"I haven't heard anything about P.D. yet," C-Sharp said.

"You are beginning to annoy me," Phillips told C-Sharp.

"Preston Demarest had already come into the picture," Michaelson said. He then explained the CIA's use of Aldrich Ames to funnel disinformation to the Soviet Union.

"Are you saying Preston had also been used as a conduit to Ames?" Catherine asked.

"No. With the Ames scandal about to go public, the CIA had to find out whether any of the people it had used with Ames had retained compromising documents or other inconvenient evidence. Demarest was recruited as a freelancer for this task, I suspect on the recommendation of Mr. Phillips. He was recruited because he was capable of exploiting Andrew Shepherd's particular sexual vulnerability. He seduced Andrew Shepherd and used the entrée this provided him to search surreptitiously for documents and records that might interest a reporter looking for a fresh angle on the Ames case. He found some."

"Lovely," Catherine said. Her voice was steady and she gazed, dry-eyed, directly at Michaelson.

"It may be aesthetically repulsive, but it was a classic operational necessity," Michaelson said. "I'm not a CIA cheerleader, but that's the reality. Information like that, promiscuously revealed, can get people killed."

"What did he find?" C-Sharp asked.

"It's not important. He found enough to realize, after Ames's arrest hit the papers, how the CIA had been using Ames. Mr. Demarest wrongly thought the CIA would view what he had as explosive information. He took it to at least two people to try to exploit the possibilities this suggested."

"Who was the other one?" Phillips asked. Catherine and Cindy both looked sharply at him.

"A man named Connaught, formerly with the CIA but now working for one of the political parties."

"The nasty little bitch *was* two-timing me, after all," Phillips confirmed with a show of indignant petulance.

"Connaught and Mr. Phillips here were both smarter than Demarest," Michaelson said. "They realized that the CIA exposé Demarest thought he had was worthless, but

184

that without knowing it Demarest was in fact onto something of genuine potential value."

"Namely?" Catherine asked.

"Documentary proof that an eighteenth-century ancestor of Marcus Humphreys was a black slaveowner. Demarest had found an arguably compromising hotel receipt hidden in one of the estate books. To take a picture of it, he had laid the receipt over the page where it was stashed. That page happened to be an indenture showing the sale of a slave to Thaddeus Praisegod Humphreys."

"Two hundred years ago?" C-Sharp squealed in amazement.

"Yes," Michaelson said. "Before the Beatles."

"How could anyone think that was politically important?"

"Oh, don't be such a *complete* twit," Phillips said impatiently. "This is a country that spent two bloody months on the verge of a shooting war and only news junkies knew about it because the lead story was a White House intern who licked something besides postage stamps in the Oval Office."

"At any rate," Michaelson said, "Connaught and our friend Phillips here each, independently, sent Demarest back into Calvert Manor to get a complete copy of the indenture that he had inadvertently photographed in partially concealed form."

"He got in the first time by seducing my father," Catherine said with a sad little head shake. "And the second time by seducing me."

"Yes," Michaelson said. "With a little help from each of his sponsors. Phillips, rather charmingly if you like that kind of thing, briefed him on a collection of harmless eccentrics called the Stuart Restoration Society."

"Don't ask," Cindy said as C-Sharp opened his mouth.

"I fell for it like a twelve-year-old with her first romance novel," Catherine said.

"Connaught chose a more sinister course. Some recent CIA appointees are much more susceptible than they should be to partisan political leverage. That explains some of the more colorful characters who've found their way into the president's company over the last few years. Connaught exploited that susceptibility to have someone there obtain the records of Catherine's psychological counseling and provide them to him. He used them to draw Demarest a road map."

"Excuse me," Willie said, rising. "If it's all right, I'm going to go set up the electronics."

"Demarest in this fashion found his way back into Calvert Manor. In the small hours of one morning he snuck into the library and got to work. After he'd found the page but before he could start clicking his Minox, Cindy interrupted him. The ensuing verbal fracas woke up Catherine. Demarest couldn't explain himself. He staged a melodramatic exit followed by a fake suicide attempt that played skillfully and mercilessly on Catherine's past trauma. The result was a reconciliation that enabled him to come back and, eventually, try again for the critical document."

"But he couldn't come up with it," Marjorie said, "because Cindy took it out of the estate book and hid it."

"He was never able to find the document again," Michaelson said as he glanced at his watch. "But he died trying. Which is what we're here to explore."

The phone rang. Catherine excused herself to answer it, returning in less than a minute.

"It's an AT&T operator for you," she told Michaelson. "She says your conference call is ready."

Twenty-three

Where's Willie?" C-Sharp asked as he looked around the living room.

"In the upstairs study, where the trustee was the day Preston bought it," Willie said, his voice resonating over a speakerphone resting next to a television monitor set up on the living-room writing table. The second-floor floor plan filled the monitor's screen.

"And who's the stiff calling in from outside?" C-Sharp said with a nod toward the speakerphone.

"Corbin James Connaught, joining us from his office in downtown Washington," Michaelson said. "Welcome to the party, Mr. Connaught."

"Joining you from my office on a Sunday morning, soon to be a Sunday afternoon," Connaught said. "Could we please get on with it?"

"I should mention that Mr. Connaught is participating reluctantly in our little exercise," Michaelson said. "I have something he wants and I'm not going to talk to him about it unless he shares this experience with us first."

187

"Perhaps you should explain what the exercise is," Catherine's voice said over the speakerphone.

"Fair enough," Michaelson said. "Mr. Connaught, through some intermediaries, gets credit for the theory that Preston Demarest's death was either accidental or an elaborately disguised suicide. Though quite implausible, the theory has the virtue of not being flatly impossible—which appears to be more than we can say for the alternative possibility of intentional homicide."

"Since our talk the other night, in other words," C-Sharp said, "we have gotten exactly, let's see, humpty-humpty, left at the light—nowhere. Zero progress. Right?"

"That's what we're here to find out," Michaelson said. "The idea is to replicate the setup at Calvert Manor the day Preston Demarest died. Catherine and Cindy Shepherd are on the phones in their bedrooms, where they were that day. Marjorie Randolph is on the extension in the downstairs den. Avery Phillips and Project are on the phone in the kitchen. Mr. Connaught is joining us from a remote location, just as Mrs. Shepherd was on the day of the killing. And Willie is taking the place of the trustee. The rest of us are in the living room."

"To what end?" Connaught asked with a sigh that the speakerphone seemed to amplify.

"To see if it is physically possible for someone taking part in this phone call on the second floor of this house to get from where they are to the room where Demarest died, stay there long enough to have killed him the way he was killed, exit while leaving behind only doors locked from the other side, and get back to the starting point, without leaving more than five minutes between their documented contributions to the call."

"Good luck," Connaught said without enthusiasm.

"Thank you," Michaelson said, scribbling on a legal pad. "It is now eleven forty-three A.M. Are you there, Willie?"

"Sure am."

"All right. Go."

"What's he doing?" Connaught asked.

"If he's following the script," Michaelson said, "he's climbing out the window onto the porch roof. You do have your copy of the floor plan, don't you?"

"Yes. Arrived by messenger yesterday morning."

"You're saying the trustee killed P.D.?" C-Sharp demanded incredulously.

"No. I'm saying someone on the second floor killed him. We can't say who, so we'll start with the position farthest away from him."

"Heee-re's Willie," a musical contralto sang then over the phone.

"Eleven forty-six," Michaelson said, making a note. "Where are you, Willie?"

"Still on the roof, outside the sewing room that's right next to the guest room where Preston went to his final reward."

"And how is it you're still able to chat with us?"

"I reached through the window of that room, picked up the receiver of an extension phone from a table near the window in there, and pulled it out here to the porch. Now I'm going a few feet down the porch to the window of the room where Preston died."

"But you can't get in through there," C-Sharp said. "At least you couldn't on the day of the killing."

"He doesn't have to get in through that window," Michaelson said. "Tell us this, Willie: Is the opening wide enough for you to stick the receiver into the room?"

"Sure is," Willie said. "And I'm just about to do it."

"Eleven forty-seven," Michaelson said. "So. Thus far our trustee stand-in has made it through about ten percent of the task without an excessive interval. Of course, this is the easy part. What Willie's doing now, with the receiver

189

safely stashed in the death room, is scooting further along the roof to the window of the bathroom on the other side. He'll enter the bathroom through that window, go through the adjoining door into the room where Demarest was, pick up the phone, and report in."

Silence intervened long enough to become noticeable. Michaelson saw everyone in the living room glance at their watches. Phillips finally broke in.

"I'm surprised you don't have elevator music playing while we're on hold," he said.

"I'll remember that for our next homicide investigation," Michaelson promised.

"An interesting experiment, I suppose," Connaught said then after another quiet period. "But if this had happened on the day in question, don't you think Demarest would have noticed little details like the open window on a cold day, the receiver dangling through that window, and so forth?"

"I'm quite certain he would have. And did."

"And it didn't strike him as a bit odd?"

"Not in the least," Michaelson said. "He thought he knew exactly why all this rigmarole was being gone through. He was collaborating actively with the killer to get her into his room."

"For the most obvious of reasons, you're implying," Connaught said.

"The obvious will do for now," Michaelson said. "We'll hold the subtleties in reserve, in case we need them later on."

"Okay, here I am," Willie panted over the phone at this point. "But getting through that window was a literal pain in the butt. Literal. You heard it here first."

"Eleven-fifty," Michaelson announced. "We could even stretch a point and call it eleven forty-nine and a half."

"Speaking of points," Phillips said, "I think you've

made yours about the phones. The conference call isn't an alibi for anyone on the second floor. Using the extension phone in the room on one side and the window of the bathroom on the other, and assuming Demarest's cooperation, the killer could have gotten from her assigned position into the room where Demarest was without being off the conference call for more than three minutes."

"Exactly," Michaelson said. "And we can all agree, I hope, that once the killer was in the room with the extension receiver, she could interject occasional comments into the conference call during brief breaks from doing whatever her purpose required. She'd have to keep the receiver under a pillow or something in between comments, lest it pick up any stray vocables. But that wouldn't be any big trick."

"I'll also stipulate that whoever it is you have up there could reverse his course, making comments within the same time limits," Connaught said. "So why don't you call this little bit of community theater a success and wrap it up?"

"Because we've handled the phones but not the exit," Michaelson said. "For that part, unfortunately, we can't simulate conditions on the day of the murder perfectly. The temperature then was twenty-two and today it's around fifty. If you'll all bear with me, though, I believe I've thought of a way around that. Willie will let you know when I step on stage again."

Michaelson left the living room for the kitchen, where Phillips glanced at him with quizzical bemusement. He pulled his Thermos from the freezer, opened it, and extracted several Baggies. Phillips couldn't tell what was inside, beyond noting that it was roughly as transparent as the Baggies themselves. Hustling a bit in deference to the understandable impatience of everyone else involved, Michaelson went upstairs and headed for the room where Demarest had died.

Cindy accosted him in the hall, cutting in front of him and slapping his chest roughly with the heels of both hands.

"Is this your idea of keeping your word?" she whispered fiercely. "Who do you think you're fooling with that any-one-of-the-three-could-have-done-it crap? You might as well accuse Cathy by name."

"I've kept my word and my conscience is clear," Michaelson said. "Now please get out of my way before someone overhears *you* accusing your sister."

As he brushed past her, she grabbed at his left arm. He swung it briskly free and with a back chop landed an elbow on her bicep, just hard enough to make her think twice about grabbing him again. He made it into the room without further interference.

"Intermission is over," Willie announced over the phone. "Enter Michaelson stage left, with Baggies."

"You're doing fine," Michaelson said. "Just keep describing exactly what I'm doing."

"Okay. He's fiddling with the lock on the bathroom door now. He just pushed the button to make the bolt spring out. . . . Now he's pushing the bolt back in. . . . He's taking a small ice cube out of the Baggie and trying to force it into the hole where the bolt is. . . . Doesn't look like it's working . . . He's getting a little frustrated . . . trying it again with a new bitty ice cube. . . . Hmm. Seems happier with this one. . . . Now he's going into the bathroom and closing the door behind him."

Michaelson exited the bathroom through its other door and trotted downstairs with an almost unbecoming spring in his step. He caught himself humming and barely managed to stop before he reached the living room.

"Thank you for your patience, everyone," he said as he got within range of the speakerphone.

"At the risk of seeming peevish," Phillips said, "so what?"

"A fair question," Michaelson answered. "By way of answer, let me ask Willie to go over and open the bathroom door without touching the lock."

"Yo, massa," Willie said, with more than the hint of a world-weary sigh in his voice. "Cord won't reach. Back in a sec."

Only a moment or two of electronic silence had passed before they heard Connaught, talking more to himself than to the rest of them.

"Pan Am 103," he murmured. "Son of a bitch."

Before anyone could follow up on this cryptic comment, Willie came back on.

"Can't do it, sports fans," he said in an uncharacteristically earnest tone. "That door be locked."

"Hold it, Willie," Phillips said. "You mean to say that Michaelson went through the doorway into the bathroom, closed the door behind him, and now it's locked from *your* side?"

"Thass right, boss," Willie said in something much closer to his customary mocking trill. "There's enough daylight between the door and the jamb to slip a quarter through, and I saw the bolt."

"How'd you do it?" C-Sharp asked.

"The ice cube, you moron," Connaught said. "The spring on the bolt must be very weak, with plenty of play in the housing."

"Well, it would be, wouldn't it?" Catherine interjected a trifle defensively, as if she were still trying to sell the house. "It's about sixty years old."

"Michaelson tripped the bolt, then manually pushed it back into the housing and held it there by jamming a small ice cube into the housing in front of it," Connaught said. "He closed the door. In the time it took him to come downstairs the ice cube melted and the bolt shot through. It's the same basic trick the terrorists who blew up Pan Am 103 over Scotland used as the timing device on the laptop computer they booby-trapped."

"So the murderer could have done the same thing," Phillips said.

"Killer, not murderer," Michaelson said. " 'Kill' is an empirical observation. 'Murder' is a legal conclusion."

"Except for one thing," Willie said. "At the risk of being a spoilsport. On the day Demarest died there's no way the killer waltzed into the kitchen and scored any Baggie full of ice chips out of the fridge. Project and I were in the kitchen, and it didn't happen."

"The killer hardly needed a freezer for her small ice cubes when she had a roof exposed to twenty-two-degree temperatures right outside her window," Michaelson said.

"All right," Connaught said. "You've provided a theoretical alternative to suicide or accident as the explanation for Demarest's death. You've shown the hypothetical possibility of any one of three people killing him. Good show and all that, but which one of them are you saying did it?"

"That's precisely the point," Michaelson said. "Our experiment provides no basis for picking any one of the three."

"Then would you be good enough to explain exactly why you have wasted going on forty-five minutes of my time?" Connaught snapped.

"In order to blackmail you," Michaelson said cheerfully. "What?"

"You see, neither Cindy Shepherd nor Catherine Shepherd had any motive for murdering Demarest. Catherine was in love with him, and Cindy viewed him as an ally in

194

her campaign to unload Calvert Manor. That leaves the trustee."

"Who likewise didn't have any motive, at least that I know of," Connaught said.

"She may or may not," Michaelson said. "It may even be that you weren't using her to try to get your hands on the document you were convinced was secreted at Calvert Manor, just as you used Demarest and tried to use me. None of that makes the slightest difference."

"It seems to make all the difference in the world to me," Connaught said.

"I'll spell it out for you," Michaelson said. "If Demarest's death wasn't a Shepherd family affair, then it was related to something else. The only something else in the picture right now is the pursuit of that document. You are deeply implicated in that pursuit. You sent Demarest in here after it, doing a great deal of psychological harm in the process. Then you put political muscle on a federal agency to force a cockeyed accident/suicide theory down the throat of the local police. So when the conspiracy theorists light up the Internet, your ears will be burning. And when enough discreet leaks from reliable sources finally generate attention from the respectable media, you'll be in the crosshairs."

"Reliable sources like who?"

"Like me," Michaelson said. "If there's any real-world possibility that a non-Shepherd killed Preston Demarest, then you are tied to a very mediagenic homicide. You won't be contributing usefully to any political party's electoral prospects. Instead, you can expect to be dividing your time for the next three years between congressional committees and grand juries."

"Are you threatening me?" Connaught demanded.

"Yes, Mr. Connaught, I am threatening you," Michaelson said with jovial firmness. "In diplomacy we call it an ultimatum. You will disengage forthwith from Calvert Manor and everything and everyone connected with it. You will stop pursuing the document you've been after. You will not send any more minions into the lives of these people in search of that document or in search of anything else. You will never again use Andrew Shepherd's name or his modest but selfless services to his country to advance any partisan or personal goal. You will, in short, leave the Shepherd family alone. Because if you don't I guarantee you I will get this story media play that will make Vince Foster's suicide and Monica Lewinsky's love life seem like page eight filler."

Five seconds that seemed like thirty passed. Then Connaught's voice came over the speakerphone again.

"And if I comply with these conditions, you'll keep quiet?"

"Yes. For a price."

"Namely?"

"Call me tomorrow at ten and we'll discuss it."

Michaelson pushed a button and the conference call ended.

The living room began to fill a bit as those who had been in other parts of the house drifted in. When Michaelson noticed that Willie and Catherine had both joined the group, he made his way over to them.

"That was fascinating," Catherine said in an oddly detached voice, as if Michaelson had just staged *Death of a Salesman* in drag. "Marjorie explained almost everything else when she called me a couple of days ago, but the ice cubes came as a surprise."

"Thank you," Michaelson said. "Speaking of ice cubes, if you'll excuse me for a moment, I'm going to run up and get what's left of them before they make a mess."

When he reached the bathroom where he'd thrown the Baggies in the sink, he found Cindy waiting for him, eyes flashing and arms folded across her chest. This did not surprise him.

"At least now we know how much your word is worth," she said bitterly. "The trustee. Of all the unmitigated bullshit."

"Ageism pure and simple," Michaelson said, shaking his head sadly. "You mean you can't see our somewhat over-weight, solidly middle-aged trustee squirming through windows and scrambling nimbly around on rooftops?"

"That cow?" Cindy demanded derisively. "As if. Plus, how could she plan on getting past either my window or Cathy's without being spotted? Never mind why Demarest would have let her fat ass into the room with him."

"Those are potential difficulties with the trustee theory," Michaelson admitted. "You'll notice I was careful not to commit myself to it."

" 'Commit'? You told everyone on that call that Cathy killed Demarest, as clearly as if you'd said it in so many words."

"I did nothing of the kind," Michaelson said. "I haven't told anyone that Catherine Shepherd killed Preston De-marest, and I never intend to. For the excellent reason that she didn't kill him. You did."

Twenty-four

I'm sure you could have seduced Demarest without the cigars, but they were a nice aesthetic touch," Michaelson said. "The kind of subtle allusion to Janos that would appeal to him."

" 'Sometimes a cigar is just a cigar,' " Cindy said. "Freud."

"It must have been particularly satisfying for you to imagine him tumbling at the last moment to the way you'd conned him, realizing as he lay there with you straddling him that he'd been had and there was nothing he could do about it—just before you slammed his head onto the stone and turned important parts of his brain into jelly."

"Are you seriously accusing me of murder based on psychobabble about cigars?" Cindy asked. Her voice betrayed no anger. Just mild amusement seasoned with a grain or two of genuine interest.

"Of course not," Michaelson answered. "Proving how he was killed effectively proves who killed him as well. Scooting through windows and over roofs was the work

198

of a former gymnast, not a former debater. You, not Catherine. And you were the one who maneuvered him into the guest room, which is the only room where this elaborate murder would have worked."

"You're forgetting that Preston had a vote," Cindy said. "I was all by myself on keeping him off that call. I couldn't have forced the issue if he hadn't gone along with it himself."

"You prearranged that with him. He played along with the skit so that you and he could end up together in that room without anyone else knowing about it, and he could get what he wanted from you."

Cindy looked contemplatively over Michaelson's left shoulder for four seconds, as if trying to analyze his argument objectively.

"Doesn't work," she said then, shaking her head. "This isn't the fifties. Grown-ups don't have to go to that kind of trouble to get laid. Besides, Preston's poofter quotient was about eighty percent. Janos was his idea of steak. Anyone with two X chromosomes was parsley at best. And when Preston did feel like some Venus action, he still didn't need me. He could get it from Cathy with half the hassle and none of the attitude."

"You didn't finesse him into that room hustle by offering him sex. You seduced him well before the killing to try to protect Catherine by enticing him to abandon her so he could go after you. He collaborated with you to get you alone in the guest room with him because you promised him that bloody indenture."

"I could have gotten the indenture to him anytime I wanted to without any cloak-and-dagger routine."

"If you'd just turned it over to him, you couldn't have enforced the promise you extracted from him in exchange for it—namely, that he'd break off the engagement to Catherine and get out of her life. You knew he'd break his word without compunction. So you told him he could get the document only by putting himself in what my sainted parents would have called a compromising situation with you: alone together in a bedroom with his pants down and your skirt up."

"I know what 'compromising situation' means," Cindy said with an eye-rolling sigh.

"Demarest thought he had you outfoxed. He went along with your demand, figuring that if you did contrive to have the two of you discovered, he could get back into Catherine's good graces by doing the same suicidal-lover-on-the-brink routine he'd worked before. But he underestimated you as badly as he overestimated himself. Once you got his pants around his ankles in that room, you had no intention of giving him anything except a dent in the back of his head and two lungs full of smoke."

"You really going to try to sell that crock to the police?" Cindy asked amiably.

"No. The police haven't helped me figure out the euro, so I feel no compulsion to help them figure out what happened to Preston Demarest. The police are the least of your worries."

"Then I guess we don't need to be having this conversation."

"Wrong," Michaelson said. "Avery Phillips is a different matter altogether. He's one of those inconvenient people who believes in certain things, and one of them is honor. He despised Preston Demarest in many ways. But when he died, Demarest was in this house in collaboration with Phillips, carrying out a plan that Phillips put together. Avery Phillips isn't going to shrug off Demarest's death because of some fairy tale about autoerotic misadventure and national security."

"Then please tell him I didn't do it," Cindy said, her

voice a trifle bored. "Or Cathy. Meanwhile, I'll watch my back."

"I'll tell him no such thing. Even if I could lie well enough to fool Phillips on something as clear as this, I'd save that talent for people who could make me secretary of state. That leaves you a bit short in the minimum-bid department."

"So you're going to finger me for him?"

"You've fingered yourself far more effectively than I ever could. If he asks me to confirm his suspicion that you killed Demarest, I will. Not because I want him to hurt you, but in the hope that then he'll listen when I explain why you killed him. That's about the only useful contribution I can still make."

"I was wondering when you'd get to motive," Cindy said. "Since as far as I know I didn't have one."

"Your motive was to safeguard Catherine," Michaelson said. "You've been fanatically protective of her since your parents' divorce and especially since she surprised your father in flagrante. You've convinced yourself that she lives her life on the edge of neurasthenia, and that you're the only thing standing between her and institutionalization. An adolescent who offered her a marijuana cigarette got an elbow in the kidneys. Preston Demarest got a fireplace stone in the back of the head."

"Right. To fiercely protect her, I killed the man she loved. Nice try."

"The man she loved but who didn't love her. You killed Preston Demarest because he was a manipulative sadist who'd exploit Catherine's neuroses and psychic trauma to get whatever he wanted. When you couldn't seduce him away from her, you killed him."

"You make it sound so noble I almost wish I'd done it just so I could try on the halo," Cindy said.

"What you did wasn't noble. You converted Demarest

from a criminal into a martyr and risked destroying Catherine's emotional balance past any hope of recovery. Good intentions aren't enough. Killing Demarest was a tragically reckless and misguided exercise in moral egotism."

"Whoa," Cindy said. "We're getting a little judgmental here, aren't we?"

"A generational habit to which I'm partial," Michaelson said icily. "Ignoble though it was, however, your killing of Demarest wasn't evil in the way that his psychological abuse of Catherine was. Legally, what you did was cold-blooded, premeditated murder. Morally, in your own judgment, it was justifiable homicide. That judgment was wrong, but your mistake was selfless rather than malicious, and your victim was someone who won't be missed. That's the idea that I hope to sell to Avery Phillips."

"You have sold it," Phillips said.

Michaelson and Cindy both looked up, startled. Phillips, who had apparently been standing in the hall, walked to the doorway and leaned against the jamb. He shifted his gaze from Michaelson to Cindy, and Michaelson watched the two of them eye each other for a moment in cool and intrigued appraisal.

"A weekend with me and I'll bet you wouldn't be gay anymore," Cindy said. Phillips shook his head.

"Tried that in high school," he said. "The third time a girl I was going with went on a crying jag because it was a cloudy day I thought, I don't need this. I'm going to date happy people who dress well. Been gay ever since. Besides, I couldn't stand the thought of Preston laughing at me in hell when I met him there after you managed to kill me the same way you did him."

"I didn't kill anyone," Cindy said.

"Stick with that denial," Phillips said. "Not that you'll need it much more. I'm walking away from this, and I'll square things with Janos. Which leaves you and Catherine, and frankly, I wouldn't touch that with Krafft-Ebbing on a stick. Maybe you two can stand in the corner together or something."

"Catherine spent this morning proving that she's stronger than anyone except Marjorie thought she was," Michaelson said. "Perhaps what she needs is someone for her to protect, instead of someone protecting her. If so, she has it now."

"Oh, dear," Phillips said, "caring nurturers at twelve o'clock. I feel a glucose OD coming on. By the way, you're about thirty seconds away from your next phone call, so I'd toddle on downstairs if I were you."

"Gracious," Michaelson said, glancing at his watch as he hurried out of the bathroom, "you're right. I hadn't really built this little dialogue into the schedule."

Trailed by Phillips, Michaelson hustled to the stairs and got back to the living room just in time to hear a female voice call his name over the speakerphone.

"This is Richard Michaelson," he said.

"Please hold for Congressman Humphreys."

Several seconds passed before a male voice came over the speaker.

"We ready to go on TV?" the voice asked.

The mumble in the background was apparently affirmative, for after a couple of flickers the monitor at Calvert Manor came to life to show Humphreys's torso, with his head pinning a telephone receiver to his shoulder.

"Thank you for calling, Congressman," Michaelson said.

"You're welcome. You've done me a considerable service, and all you asked in return was a phone call, so I thought I should oblige. I'm on a speaker, right? Who all we have there?"

Michaelson inventoried the crowd.

"Okay," Humphreys said. "Well, I got the copy of that

document you had couriered to my office. Where's the original, if you don't mind my asking?"

"With an archival document preservation expert at George Washington University."

"Sounds like a real good place for it."

"We rigged a television hookup for this call so that you could look at the book the document came out of, in case you have any doubts about its authenticity."

"I don't," Humphreys said. "We're going straight up the middle with this. Press release hits the wire in fifteen minutes. Speech and press conference in less than three hours. Finding out that thing's a forgery would spoil a real good strategy."

"Preemptive disclosure," Michaelson said, nodding.

"Now, that's what *I* called it," Humphreys said, grinning. "What my staff tells me is that we're being 'proactive.' It's like Chick Johnson in that old vaudeville routine: We're not confessing, we're bragging."

"I'll leave the semantics in your more than capable hands," Michaelson said.

"Seriously," Humphreys said then, "if this thing had blindsided us three weeks before an election, we'd have been running for cover. This way we get to lead with it, turn it into a positive. The only way I could get more coverage on a Sunday afternoon is to be assassinated."

"That strikes me as too high a price to pay for a Monday-morning headline," Michaelson said. "Good luck with it."

Humphreys leaned back in his chair and seemed to relax a bit. His expression became more reflective, as if the journeyman pol thrilling helpful amateurs with inside banter about tactics had suddenly yielded the floor to a serious thinker.

"Funny thing," he said. "I've known at least since college that there were black slaveowners, although it never occurred to me that my own ancestors might have been among them. I don't know of any serious historians who even question it. But all the same, that piece of paper would've been a world-class bombshell at the climax of a campaign. Even some kids on my own staff were stunned by it. They *didn't* know. They'd never even thought about it."

"I suspect most people haven't," Michaelson said.

"Most people haven't thought, period," Humphreys said. "There are tens of millions of voters out there whose *total* idea of American slavery comes from seeing *Roots* or *Gone With the Wind*. They have no idea that there were any blacks before the Civil War who weren't slaves, or that there were whites opposing slavery while Abe Lincoln was still learning his ABC's. They buy what I say about health insurance regulation or transportation policy because they want to square things with Kunta Kinte. That indenture is going to mess with their heads. And if you're going to mess with people's heads, it's better to be on offense than on defense."

"So now they'll get a little real history on television," Michaelson said.

"Very little, but very real," Humphreys said. "Okay, now you know the game plan. Was that all you had for me?"

"That's it."

"Then thanks again for handling it the way you did, and check CNN at three o'clock Eastern."

The screen went blank and the line went dead. Michaelson stared for a moment at the monitor.

"He was right," Marjorie commented. "One hundred percent of what many Americans know about slavery comes from television."

"Yes," Michaelson said. "Just like one hundred percent of what I know, even now, about Marcus Humphreys. Even when we had a direct conversation, the dominant image I have of him is from a television screen."

"Kind of messy, isn't it?" Phillips said quietly to them, nodding toward Cindy and Catherine across the room. "Just leaving them this way. The killer and the neurotic. Lizzie Borden and Martha Stewart, playing house."

"I suppose so," Michaelson said. "They're collateral damage. Like those kids whose legs are blown off by land mines years after the fighting is over. We were at war and we won, but the price of victory included innocent lives."

"Catherine didn't have a chance before," Marjorie said. "Maybe she has a chance now. That's something."

"Not much," Phillips said.

"A small thing," Michaelson agreed. "But all there is. Thanks for providing the electronics. I'd pitch in on packing it up, but I'd probably break something."

"Don't bother," Phillips said. "Just answer one more question."

"Shoot."

"What are you going to demand from Connaught when he calls tomorrow?"

"A medal," Michaelson said.

Twenty-five

"I was delighted to get Willie a ticket for this," Michaelson whispered to Marjorie eleven weeks later. "But I can't imagine why he wanted to come."

"Soaking up atmosphere," Marjorie said. "He's working on a movie script."

"Seriously?"

"Yes indeed. A thriller revolving around a politically sensitive document hidden in a crate of German sausage."

"Remarkable," Michaelson said. "A wurst-case scenario."

"That's his title."

They shut up then and rose because a stentorian voice said, "Ladies and gentlemen, the President of the United States."

The president was in good form, as usual. The setting helped. The East Room of the White House, the seal on the podium, the reporters and camcorders crowding the seats, the flags, the sunshine from the Rose Garden window, the marine guards in dress blues. It all conspired to produce just the right pitch of understated solemnity.

The lists of accomplishments for each of the seven people behind him had certainly been written by someone else, certainly not been glimpsed by the presidential eye until minutes before he stepped to the rostrum. Yet he read it as if he'd penned every syllable himself. Now he'd reached the climax of the ceremony.

"And so it is my high honor and distinct privilege to recognize the remarkable contributions of each of these distinguished Americans with our nation's highest civilian decoration, the Presidential Medal of Freedom," he said. "First, James Terence Halliburton."

A discreet attendant pushed Halliburton's wheelchair forward. Halliburton wore a lustrous navy blue suit, a white shirt, and a blue silk tie with broad red diagonal stripes. Blue-faced cuff links stamped in silver with the seal of the United States Department of State showed just below his coat sleeves. His black wingtips had been buffed to a mirrorlike shine. Every strand of his thinning hair was in place. If you hadn't heard him chatting a few minutes before the ceremony about how Nixon couldn't be counted out, you might confidently have sent him into a negotiation over anything from fishing rights to hostages.

Smiling warmly, the president leaned over the wheelchair and pinned the medal to Halliburton's left lapel. Shutters snapped. Electronic flashes flashed. The president spoke a few confidential words, getting heaven knew what response from Halliburton. Then he shook the older man's hand amidst more snaps and flashes and stepped back to the podium.

That was it. Michaelson studied Halliburton's eyes intently during the exchange, hoping desperately to spot some flicker of lucidity, however brief, some precious interval of understanding. And he saw one. He was sure of it. He wasn't given to kidding himself and he felt confident of his judgment.

He sat back in his folding chair, satisfied. It was a small thing, done well.

Author's Notes

The historical premise underlying *Collateral Damage* is accurate. Free persons of color lived and worked in Maryland and elsewhere in the antebellum South, and in some cases they owned slaves and exploited the labor of those slaves in the same way that white slaveowners did. As one detailed treatment of the subject explains:

> Although the academic community is fully aware that there were Afro-American slave masters, their existence is not common knowledge among the public. Most Americans, black and white, believe that slavery was a system exclusively maintained by whites to exploit black people. But in fact Afro-Americans played a small yet significant role in the annals of the peculiar institution as slave masters. Many black Americans of the antebellum period believed that slavery was a viable economic system and exploited the labor of black people for profit. In Louisiana,

Maryland, South Carolina, and Virginia, free blacks owned more than 10,000 slaves, according to the federal census of 1830.

Larry Kroger, *Black Slaveowners: Free Black Slave Masters in South Carolina, 1790–1860* (University of South Carolina Press, 1985), 1.

The story's technical premise is also authentic. The exit method demonstrated by Michaelson was empirically verified by physical experiment before publication. Readers who would like to examine time-lapse photographs documenting the experiment may obtain them without charge by sending a stamped, self-addressed envelope to Cold Coast Productions, P.O. Box 510015, Milwaukee, WI 53202. Readers who would like to examine a videotape documenting the experiment may obtain it by sending a check or money order in the amount of $15 to the same address.